Gettin' In The Game

by Bossy Lioness

I0548241

Cover Curated by Deanna M. Morgan

Cover Art completed by Keith Wesson

I guess it's true when they say everything that's done in the dark always comes to the light. *But damn, I would have never thought that it would be like this!*

I had been on the morning shift for the last three months, finally getting back to a regular schedule. Joanie came to me asking-practically begging me to switch with her and work overnight for her so she could go to this all-white affair with *Kelly, Marvie and Rhonda.* She said she was only pressed because she heard Herb, her boyfriend talking about it to his homie. Man, please that's one thing I don't miss-stalking a dude to make sure he not out here playing me. Those days were over. Fuck that! I had my share of playing deaf, dumb and blind all for a couple of dollars and dick. But, I'm not even going to front, the dick *was* good and the money *was* aiight! It was way past time to ante up though and play the game these niggas always playing.

Not only did I get in the game, shit, I was winning like a muthafucka! A few weeks back, more like three months ago, I was leaving the Day Spa for my monthly 'queen for a day' special. You know, a mani, pedi, a massage and that good ole chin wax. I had two glasses of their complimentary wine so a sister was feeling nice. On the way to my car, some dude spoke to me and I gave him a little smile but didn't open my mouth to speak. He said to me *"nice smile, I wonder if that voice match that nice smile of yours"*. I brushed him off with a little *"thanks"*. I was not interested in whatever bullshit conversation he was trying to get into. He was like *'damn shorty, it's like that?'* I continued to my car and didn't bother to notice which way the dude had went. Once in my car, I pulled out my phone to call Haasan but he didn't answer. I instantly redialed him because I was trying to plan how the rest of my day off was going to go.

Since he didn't answer, I figured I head to Longhorn's to get some of my favorite firecracker wraps because I was hungry. I was at the gym early in the morning before going to the spa and had worked up an appetite. Not to mention those two glasses of wine and I know how I am. I am a lightweight, never been one to be able to hold my liquor. I thought about ordering takeout, but shit I mind as well dine-in since I didn't have anything to do at the moment. I usually sit at the bar, but today I chose a booth. I ordered my food and while I waited I scrolled through my emails to see if I had any price drop alerts on any of the many things I had been trying to buy. Yep, I am a certified shopaholic- but on a budget. I may splurge once in a while on something I think that I just have to have. As much as I love nice things, I don't like to spend a lot of money on them. Haasan calls me cheap, but hardly. Between what I make and all the money that he loves to give me I still try to spend wisely. I call it being economical.

I hadn't been sitting too long when the waiter came back with my food. I was happy. I ate that food so fast like somebody was going to take it from me. That's one of the reasons I wanted the booth today, I needed privacy because the way my stomach was growling I knew I was going to demolish those firecracker wraps. I asked for another water and the check. To my surprise the waiter told me that my bill had been paid by the guy in the light green polo at the bar. Now, the guy's back was turned to me but I knew it wasn't Haasan, because he is a caramel complexion. I thanked the waiter and walked over to the bar and saw that it was the guy who had spoke to me as I was leaving the Spa. I said to him as his back was turned *"I don't know whether to be thankful or scared"*. He turned around with all his bright whites showing, smiling and said *"you're welcome."* Now, I did not get a good look at this dude earlier but when I tell you he was Fine with a capital fucking F! He was Wesley Snipes dark with jet black hair that was like an ocean. Now, it's been a long time that a nigga besides Haasan made my stomach flutter and my panties wet on site. But this man right here did just that. I replied, trying not to show how taken aback I was at his fucking beauty by saying *"I don't believe I said thank you just yet. And, what the hell, are you following me?"* I swear I tried hard not to gaze into his eyes as he talked.

He laughed and was like *"Naw, I wasn't following you. I'm waiting for my man so I sat here at the bar to get a drink and I saw you sitting over there fucking up your food. I was going to come over but shit, I didn't want to interrupt you. You was over there handling your business".*

I guess I should have been embarrassed but I wasn't, I laughed and simply said, *"Shiddd, thank you because a sister was hungry as hell! It was the first thing I ate today and I probably would have been irked if you did come and bother me".*

He said, *"Well, at least I got to finally hear your voice. You act like you didn't want to speak earlier. And, your voice isn't what I expected, it's better".*

I said *"yeah, yeah, thanks"*. He shook his head. I asked him why he was shaking his head.

He said *"you're a tough one, huh? What's your name?"*

I thought for a second about giving him a fake name, but to my surprise, I said *"Tovah"*.

He looked at me and said *"are you sure?"*

I was like *"what do you mean am I sure?"*

He said, *"You looked like you had to think about it before you said it"*.

I told him that I never give out my real name and that I was surprised that I had told him my real name. He laughed and said that he was glad that I did.

He said, *"Tovah, huh? That's different, it's nice."* I thanked him and asked his name.

He looked at me and said *"Sallahdeen"* almost as if I should have known who he was.

I just replied, *"Sallahdeen, huh? That's different, it's nice"*. We both laughed. I said *"well thanks for paying my bill Sallahdeen, I assume you tipped the waiter as well?"*

He said, *"Yup, I sure did. If you eat like that all the time, I'd be happy to pay your bill anytime. It's not often that a female only spends $11 when they go out to eat!"* I waved my hand and said that was grabbing a bite to eat that was not a real meal. He asked if he could take me out to dinner. I declined and told him that I have a man.

At that moment, my phone rang and it was Haasan finally calling me back. I thanked Sallahdeen again and told him goodbye. I picked up the phone and said hello but Haasan must have butt dialed me. Of course I didn't hang up, I did what any female would do- I listened. It wasn't much to listen to just him talking to someone about his car. He had just bought a brand new Infiniti QX30 SUV and was hype as hell. He had gotten it all tinted out and was proud of *'his baby'*. It was nice and all but I didn't see what the big deal was, but he loved that jawn. I hung up and I called him back and he didn't answer. The fuck. Haasan really don't be doing much but always acting like he taking care of business. I know he spend a lot of time riding around making sure everybody see his new car. I get so sick of him not spending any time with me, he swear that just because he putting money in my pocket that supposed to make up for the time he always in the streets. I make my own money so that money he giving me is just extra. I want some fucking attention and affection.

Interrupting my little thought tantrum was some light skinned nut ass dude that I know from being around the way. Dude was always corny as hell, but he had got lucky and hit the lottery for what I heard was a half a mill and came up. He driving around the hood in a 2020 Maybach s650 and always dressing like he going to a fucking cabaret. In my mind money might can make an ugly person look attractive-maybe…it just can't change corny. No matter how much money a motherfucker might have and whatever designer clothes they wear it can't disguise corny. If there was ever a doubt in my mind that it could, he deaded that shit. Anyway, he drove up with what sounds like Future blasting out of his ride. Corny. He looked at me as if I'm supposed to acknowledge him, I turned away and started my car looking for a station on my Pandora. Just then I hear him speaking to someone. It's Sallahdeen. Now I know Sallahdeen not hanging with this nut ass bol. But, shit, I don't know him. He might be just as corny as his friend. But, I didn't get corny vibes from our brief meeting.

Sallahdeen looked my way and said, *"What you was waiting for me?"*

"No, I replied and nodded my head towards the Maybach and said *"oh that's your mans?"*

He laughed shaking his head and was like *"yeah, this my bol, why?"*

I just gave him a smirk, nodding my head and said *"solid"*.

He said, *"Yo, you funny as hell, you should let me take you out to dinner later."*

Again, I surprised myself without thinking and said *"cool."*

He seemed to try to hide his surprise and was like *"oh ok, where you want to go?"*

"You asked me. What time should I be ready?"

Right on cue, he answered, *"7:30, meet me here. Don't have me waiting either".*

I repeated it back to him, *"7:30 and don't have me waiting either."*

I drove off thinking like what the fuck did I just do? I have never cheated on Haasan, I never even gave other niggas any thought. What was I doing? I guess this was me playing the game. Haasan had been slacking lately which was why I was switching my shift to mornings. He seemed to be getting too comfortable with me not being home at nights.

We didn't live together but either he stayed at the apartment or I was at his place. Basically the only times we weren't with each other is when he went out of town to take care of business or when he went upstate to visit his brother.

When I first started on nights he was bitching like crazy. I didn't like the idea of having my man sleeping alone at night, but I had waited so long to get into Jefferson Hospital and the only opening they had was in the ER on the overnights. I figured I would spend a few months-six months is what I had to do before I could put in for a transfer. Well, it had been nine months and finally some girl Joanie was leaving morning shift because she was going back to school and needed to work overnight. She knew that I wanted mornings and gave me a heads up that in six weeks classes were to begin and we could do a swap. I thanked her for the heads up but also let her know that this is what I have been waiting for—so it was for keeps and that we still would have to officially swap. She was cool with it so now I'm just waiting. When I told Haasan the good news he didn't seem too thrilled like I thought he would be. I've never been a dummy and if this nigga did find him a little side jawn, I'm about to shut all his shit down. I'm just saying. Of course you hear shit when you dealing with a pretty boy that got money. Bitches want you to think shit is going on even when it's not. I'm the type of female that needs hard evidence- I need to see shit for myself. Because sometimes you can't even trust your best friend. That's right. I had an issue back in the day with my main bitch, who I knew was a hoe, but never did I ever think the bitch would do me like she did. Fucked and sucked my man and running back to me telling me shit she either heard about or supposedly saw. Trying to create problems that weren't even there just to get some of that good dick, my good dick. And, I blame myself because she wouldn't have even known how good his dick was or how good he ate pussy-if I didn't tell her all the juicy details. Never again though. Lesson fucking learned. But I did trash the bitch, she had it coming. And, I'm not even the fighting type but sometimes people will take you there. I dumped his ass right after because even though the dick was good, I can admit now that he was corny as hell. I'll be damned if I'm going to get played by a corny dude. He was my first so I had blinders on, you know how that shit go.

Back to Haasan, yup he's a pretty boy. He is 6 foot two, caramel complexion, banging ass body with a fucking Colgate smile. Yes, my baby has an ocean too. Lately, he let his hair grow in a little on the top and he loves when I unravel the tight but soft curls when his head is in my lap. My baby is tall enough that I can look up to him and stand on my tippy toes to stretch and throw my arms around his neck and who can easily pick my five foot one frame up off the floor whenever necessary. He has abs for days and you know that thing they do when they move their chests? I fuckin' love it and I love feeling his biceps when he picks me up off my feet. My baby has also been blessed with a third leg. You got the picture? Need I say more?

It's been almost year five years that we've been together. I remember it like it was yesterday. *When they say opposites attract that was us. He was like salt and I was the slug. I met him towards the end of my first year of college. I was attending CCP (Community College of Philadelphia) and after class I had went to the Milano store on Spring Garden to grab a shirt because I heard some girl in class saying that there was a one day sale going on. Like I said before, I loves me a sale. I hated going in there though because it was always crowded. The girl who runs the shop knew what she was doing by putting her store near a college campus. I don't know if it was purposely done or coincidence but I know that jawn stay packed! So either way, it was a win for her. Anyway, I knew exactly what I was going in there for so I go grab my size and get in line. Always prepared, I pull out my phone and go to the website just in case I need a promo code to get the sale. I did, so I was glad I looked. The wait wasn't too long though, it was a few dudes off to the side upfront who I thought was in line. I guess they were waiting for somebody shopping in the store. I don't know but I was glad. When I got up to the counter, here comes one of the dudes trying to holla. Never been thirsty or looking for attention I acted like I didn't know he was talking to me. I don't know if he was really interested or trying to show off for his friends but either way he told the cashier I got this and told me to put away my money. I was like "oh, that's what up. That's your random act of kindness for today?"*

His homies laughed. He said, "Call it what you want, but I saw a pretty female and I just wanted to do something nice for her".

I said, "Okkk, well thank you".

He replied, "You're welcome".

Then I got my receipt from the cashier and walked out the store. I was half expecting him to follow me and was kind of surprised that he didn't. I walked to the subway thinking I guess he was just doing something nice. It must be nice to spend $90 on a random female. I figured he must be a drug *dealer and stunting for his friends and females is just what he did. I must admit, he was on my mind the entire time I was on the train. Even when I got to my car, I thought he had a nerve to be cute and didn't ask for my number. I put some music on finally just to stop thinking about the stranger who bought my sale items. Once DMX came on, I was in beast mode growling and shit and the nice gesture from the bol was put out of my mind.*

I came home to the smell of chicken frying. That meant Manda was home. Manda was my cousin but more like my sister. We had always been close coming up. Our dads were cousins and were thick as thieves. They were so tight that most people thought they were brothers. We had gotten even closer a few years back when both of them were killed in a drive-by. Even though it was a drive-by everybody knew it was a hit. We were young when it happened but the streets talk and even in whispers the truth wasn't going to stay hidden from us for too long. Our dads were legends in these streets, they were loved in the hood but the shit they did out of the hood made them have a bunch of enemies. Our moms were sort of tight over the years but after their men were killed they drifted. I think it was a silent blame game. Each of them blamed the other's man for them both getting killed. Our dads probably shaking their heads at them from the graves because they both made choices together that got them killed. From what I saw growing up, they had each other's backs in everything. It was kind of only right that they died together. It sounds crazy to say but if you knew them, you would probably agree.

No matter how our moms felt about the situation one thing they never tried to do was keep me and Manda apart from each other. I'm glad though because even though we were younger, we were old enough to realize that shit was changing since our dads had died. I usually use the word died when asked about my father because the moment you say the word killed- people judge him or even worse- me. My dad was a good man, a good father to me. My mom told me that a few years ago when she thought she'd school me about him and try to prepare me for the stories she knew I would hear about him and his cousin. What she didn't know is that I had already heard the stories. Some good, some bad. I appreciated her reminding me what I had already known. My dad loved me and wanted me to be unaware of the street life-of his life. From most of the stories I had heard my dad was a hood legend and a lot of the people around the way fucked with him like that. One of the early stories I heard about him was when one of the oldheads around the way had called him the real Robin Hood. It wasn't until I was older that I actually understood what he meant by that.

Manda and I shared a bond that couldn't be broken. As our dads used to say, that bond was formed while y'all were still in the womb. It was unfathomable and deliberate. The females in their lives- our mothers were made to understand that nothing would ever break their bond and that their kids would share the same bond that their parents had. And so it was. After graduating from high school, we got an apartment. Well, it was an apartment duplex that our dads had owned so we already had our own apartments just waiting for us to move in. Most people would probably love the idea of having their own place coming right out of high school but we figured we would rather live together and have money coming in by renting out the upstairs. That would take care of the bills and I could focus on school and not have to worry about finding a job. The decision made sense because me and Manda were basically inseparable anyway. One thing I can say about our dads is that they were definitely business savvy. They had bought a couple of properties and flipped them generating a nice return between the two of them. Both of our moms owned the houses that they lived in and the duplex that me and Manda currently reside in is actually ours. Both of our names are on the deed and it is paid in full. Once we found that out it was on. We had first planned that once we graduated high school that we would have our own spot in the duplex at least for a little while. My plan has always been to become a nurse (BSN). Two years commute and stay on campus for the last two years. Manda hasn't always been too clear as to what she wants to do. She is smart as hell and could probably get into whatever college she wants. But she has always been too busy being a hoe. My cousin gets all the bitches. Yeah, early on she had a boyfriend and realized right away that she got turned on more by the females than the niggas. She got turned the fuck out by her first female though. She was way out of her league with Na. Don't bring her up though. She hates to be reminded about how Na had her all fucked up. She got a bitch licking on her for the first time in her life and didn't know how to act. Na broke her heart though and fucked it up for the rest of the females. Manda went from femme to straight butch after that. She wasn't about to let another female have her like that, she wanted to be the one having bitches turned the fuck out. You can't tell her she not a dude though. And she got a nerve to be a pretty jawn at that. Long, brown hair that she keeps in either straight backs or individuals. Dress like a dude and all and she got swag. Be having these girls out here tripping. I get to see that shit upfront with us living together. Half of the stuff I witness I wouldn't believe it if I didn't see it for myself. Manda cool as hell too, real laid-back.

I hear Nicki Manaj on the speaker and rolled my eyes as I opened the door. Manda just so happened to look up and started laughing. She know damn well I don't fuck with Nicki like that so she started reciting some of the lyrics to the song. I waved my hand like please as if that would silence her. I dropped my bags and went straight to the kitchen to see if any of that chicken was done. It was already a pan ready and some more in the deep fryer. I started to yell to her not realizing she was already coming in behind me.

She was smiling and shit talking about "shit good, ain't it? Better than Popeye's?

I laughed, biting on the chicken agreeing with her "yup, shit just how I like it cousin, you know you the shit, foh. What we having a party or something, fuck all this chicken for?"

She said, "Naw, Qua and Mir coming through and you know how they get when they smoke. Eat up every fucking thing! So I just made some chicken and pasta salad for us, you...oh and I told some chick I'm trying to holla at to come through too".

I looked at her laughing while I was licking my fingers "I knew it, I knew you wasn't being all nice because of them. I knew a female had to be involved somewhere in the mix".

She rubbed her hands together and said, "You know ya cousin so well". I asked did this person have a name, she said "Kori with a K".

I walked to the sink to wash my hands and said "Okay, Kori with a K. I'll try to stay out your way. Are they all coming 'round the same time?"

She explained that she wanted Kori with a K to feel comfortable, so of course I'll be here when she gets here and she'll be there before the guys come through and after that everybody will eventually get to going, so she have some alone time with Kori with a K. That was fine with me. I had planned on relaxing the rest of the night and maybe crack open a book and do a little homework. I didn't have any classes until tomorrow evening and it was my only class of the day.

I went back to the living room and scooped up my bags and it wasn't until Manda asked me if I had gotten her anything from the Milano store that I remembered I didn't tell her what had happened. After I told her, she said the same thing I had said. That he must have been a drug dealer showing off for or whatever.

I went to my room so I could shower and get out of these clothes and get comfortable and eat some more chicken and some pasta salad. One of the advantages of living with Manda- she could cook her ass off. She got that from her mom and her dad. They both could throw down in the kitchen. I took after my mom who knows how to cook, but doesn't like to. I found that out quickly after my dad died. I

thought, you know, everyone was bringing food over at first

and Aunt Liv cooked because she liked to and because I think

she wanted to keep busy. But after a while when we were only

eating out or mom had takeout food, I asked her when was

she going to start cooking again. She told me flat out that

those days were over, I started laughing and she was dead

serious. I mean she may have cooked every now and then but

when she told me those days were over she meant it. I didn't

miss out though, I was over at Manda's house just as much

as I was home so if I wanted a home cooked meal, I knew I

would get it at Aunt Liv's. It's not that I don't like to cook

but, yeah, that's exactly it. I don't know why I was going to

try and lie. It's plain and simple, I will cook only if I have to

but why cook when I can eat out? Not very healthy I know

coming from a future nurse, but I'll worry about that in the

future- or not.

After my shower, I put on my favorite shorts and a

tank top. The shorts were my favorite because they were my dad's. They were a pair of Temple basketball shorts that he would wear around the house so when he died I took them and began wearing them. I wear them at least twice a week I don't know I guess it's a sentimental thing. I have enough memories of my dad to last a lifetime but I somehow feel close to him when I wear the shorts or even see them hanging in my closet. I grabbed my Milano bag and took out the Simba slides that I had been wanting but didn't want to pay the full price for. I put them on and they were nice and comfy. I unfolded my bodysuit just to take another look at and put it on a hanger and put it in the closet. I wasn't a fan of clothing that had writing all over it but I liked how the model had rocked it with the denim booty shorts so yup I got it. Hopefully, it won't get lost with all the other clothing with tags that are in my closet. I won't ever have to worry about not having something to wear if something comes up because I have so many unpopped tags in my closet it's a shame. Since I began school, I have been such a homebody. I need a night out so I can get cute. I got the receipt out the bag-

because as a rule for myself I keep all receipts until I wear any new piece of clothing. I don't care how long it's been, I might can't get my money back but there's always store credit. As I was about to put the receipt with the rest I noticed writing on the back of it. It was a number and a name. Haasan with two A's. But how? Did he already know he was going to pay for my stuff? When did he tell the cashier to put his number? Shit was it his number or the cashier's? I was really asking myself a bunch of questions like I was going to get an answer. I sat there looking at the name and number really trying to figure out. Then I just reached for my phone. Fuck it, my curiosity got the best of me.

I dialed the number and two rings later a guy answered saying "Who this?" I looked at the phone and hesitated. The guy said "hello?"

I finally muttered, "Hello".

The guy again said "Who this?"

I then got it together and asked, "Is this Haasan?"
He seemingly started to get irked because his question wasn't
being answered. I don't blame him, I would have been the
same way.

He then said, "Yo, who the fuck is this?!"

Finally, I answered his question. "Hi Haasan, this is
Tovah."

"Tovah, I don't know a Tovah?"

I then let him know I was the girl from the Milano
store earlier that day that he treated with the random act of
kindness.

He found that funny and laughed. He said, "Oh, hey
beautiful. I wasn't sure if you were going to call."

I had to know so I asked him how he managed to get
his name and number on the receipt without me realizing it.
It was simple really, he told me that the cashier was his
cousin and he had already had his eye on me before I got in

line and he had told her to look out and put his name and number on the receipt while he had my attention. I told him that was kind of smooth and that I called because I was curious as hell as to how he pulled it off.

He said, "oh you newsy too, huh?"

I laughed and said, "I guess I am."

"Yeah, I was betting on you to be".

We talked for a few minutes and I asked him is that how he get girls- by buying them stuff to get them to talk to him?

He said, "naw ma, that's not my m.o."

I did confess that I was a bit surprised that he didn't follow me out of the store not knowing that he had unwittingly gave me his number.

He said, "Oh, yeah? That's what's up."

I said, "why is that what's up?"

He said because it sounded like I wanted him too. I let him know that I was just surprised. The phone call lasted for only a few minutes and he told me that he has my number and asked if he could call me back later. I told him that would be cool and we said our goodbyes. I sat there replaying our brief conversation. I don't know what it was but something about him I liked. I started to go in a little zone when I heard the doorbell ring. That must be Kori with a K. I put my phone on the charger and headed out to the living room. Manda had her arms around the waist of a short, thick chocolate jawn with some long ass jet black wavy hair. You could tell it wasn't weave, her shit looked like she had Indian in her family.

Manda turned around, smiling as she introduced us. "Kori, this my cousin Tovah, Tov this is Kori". We both smiled and said hi.

Kori with a K then said, "I actually saw you earlier".

Manda and I both looked each other and I said,
"Really?" I figured she went to CCP too.

She said, "Yeah, at the Milano store". I thought like
damn she got a good memory as packed as it was in there.
She said, "I work there, I'm a cashier. I gave you a receipt
earlier with a little surprise on the back."

I laughed. Manda was looking like what fucking
surprise on the back. I said, looking mostly at Manda to clue
her in "oh, yeah, you're slick. Cuz, I didn't get a chance to
tell you that when I took my stuff out of the bag, my receipt
had a little surprise. It had a name and number on the back.
The bol I told you about? Who bought my stuff?"

Manda stood shaking her head waiting to hear the
rest. "Yeah, he had the cashier- I waved my hand towards
Kori- put his name and number on the back of the receipt. I
didn't even peep it before I put the receipt in the bag."

Manda now following, interrupted and said, "So wait,
how you know this?"

"When I finally saw the receipt, my curiosity got the best of me and I called the number" I replied.

Manda laughed, "Yo cuz, you newsy as shit."

"No, I'm just curious, thank you very much. Anyway, his name is Haasan- with two A's" I said matter-of-factly. Manda and Kori laughed.

Kori then said, "Yeah, Haasan had his eye on you as soon as you walked in the door and told me that if you got in line to put his info on your receipt." I nodded thinking that what she said was what he had told me on the phone.

Manda looked at Kori and said, "Oh you sneaky, huh?"

Kori replied back, "not at all, I was just doing a favor for my cousin." "Oh, aiight", Manda said slyly.

Changing the subject, Manda said, "What's up, y'all ready to eat? Tov, I already know. Looking at Kori she asked, "what about you sexy, I told you I got you, you ready to eat?"

Kori who looked like she was blushing, said "Yeah, I can eat something."

Ever the host with her female friends, Manda made all of our plates and we sat in the little dining area off of the kitchen. It was so quiet because we were tearing the food up, I laughed when I started to lick my fingers. They both looked up at me with their greasy lips and I said, "Alexa, play Mary J. Blige." I told them I was tired of hearing all that smacking. I guess Kori told Manda how good the food was because I heard Manda say, I told you I don't play in the kitchen." I walked back to my room to see if I had any missed calls or texts. I knew I didn't because my phone had been dry lately. I did have a text from one of my classmates asking for my notes from class today. I texted her back and told her that I would send them to her email in a few. There were a few notifications from Instagram but that's about it. I went on

Instagram to see if was anything going on and there was nothing that held my interest. I was half hoping that Haasan had called. And I definitely wasn't calling him.

A few minutes later, Qua and Mir showed up just like Manda said. When I came out my room they were already in the kitchen.

"I hope y'all washed y'all hands" I said to both of them.

They both looked at me and Mir said "now, Tov don't come at us like that".

Qua said "yes, Mom we washed our hands."

I laughed and rolled my eyes and said "just making sure, I don't know where y'all been". They didn't take offense. We all go way back. They were really Manda friends and mine by default. But because me and Manda were so close all of us were close. They were over the apartment if not every day- then most days. I got the inside scoop on all the females just by being around them. They were whores just like Manda if not bigger ones. And just like Manda, they were pretty boys. Light-skinned with pretty eyes, shit all three of them could pass as siblings if you didn't know them.

Mir said, "Alexa play Meek Mill".

Manda said, "Here you go, me and Kori listening to Mary J. and"—

Mir interrupted, "Kori, you fuck wit Meek?"

Kori looked to Manda shaking her head "yeah, I like Meek".

Mir put up his hand that was holding a piece of chicken and said, "aiight then bro, don't worry we'll be out of y'all way after this grub, right Qua?" Qua with a mouth full of food said "yup". Manda tried to look irked but we all knew she wasn't, the evening was going just to way she wanted it to go. Kori seemed to be enjoying herself too, she was all smiles listening to whatever game Manda was giving her.

As promised, Mir and Qua ate and puffed on the el that Manda had sparked up and went on their way. I retreated to my bedroom and gave Manda the privacy that she wanted with Kori. I took my notes out to send to my classmate and just as I finished my phone rang. It was Haasan. I answered and he asked me if I was free to talk. I told him I was and we talked on the phone for almost three hours.

By the end of the night, I knew that Haasan was a Scorpio, he didn't have any kids and has an older brother that was currently doing a bid upstate. He does have a niece that he's pretty close to though. Her name is Jordan, I don't remember him saying her age though. He said his brother was a huge Chicago Bulls fan so it came as no surprise when he named his firstborn Jordan. I was cracking up when he said it didn't matter if it was going to be a boy or a girl that baby's name was going to be Jordan. His brother had made that clear to his then girlfriend. I also found out that he was mixed. His mom was Asian and his dad was Black and that he was a self-proclaimed momma's boy. He had confided in me that his mom's family disowned her after she got pregnant with his brother and they found out it was by a black man. So he don't really know anyone on his mom's side of the family. The way he talked about his family sounds like they are really close. They are a little on the older side too because he said his dad was retiring and that his parents planned to take a trip that they had been talking about for years. He said that he had a girlfriend for about four years throughout high school but they had broken up after senior year. I asked him why did they break up and he said because she went away to college and he wasn't doing no long distance shit. That was two years ago and since then he said he's been living the single life.

Of course I told him about me. I told him that I was an only child and that I had always been a daddy's girl up until he died when I was twelve years old. I told him that the two people I was closest to were Manda and my mom. Noticing my backpack when I was in the Milano store he asked did I go to CCP. I told him that I did for the time being and my plan to attend Immaculata afterwards. He seemed to be impressed and asked why Immaculata. I told him that I had attended Episcopal Academy and the majority of people went there after graduation and they have a good nursing program.

"Oh, you a Catholic school chick"?

I answered, "First of all, I'm not a chick and second what is that supposed to mean"?

"Calm down shorty, I didn't mean nothing by it. But it does explain a lot".

I asked what he meant by that. He said that he had wondered how we never crossed paths and we were both from around the way. I told him that my mom kept a tight rein on me after my dad had died and getting bussed to and from school all the way out in Newtown Square, I didn't really have much time for a social life anyway.

He understood that and asked, "So, you got any ex-boyfriends, one of them Catholic school bols?" I told him that I dated a guy on and off throughout high school but it didn't work out. He said it's hard to believe that I don't have a bunch of exes still trying to holla. I told him that the guy had cheated on me with some girl that I thought was my best friend. "What about any other girlfriends?"

"Nope, I replied. Friends are overrated. I learned my lesson early. Manda is my cousin and my best friend and most of the people I'm cool with are her friends".

"Damn girl, I got to get you out of the house and show you a good time. You are too young and too fucking pretty to just go to school and go home. I got to show you how to live!"

I started laughing and said, "Well, thank you, but damn, it ain't that bad."

He said, "oh yeah, when was the last time you went on a date?" He had me there.

I said, "Uhmmm…"

He said "you gots to be fucking kidding me? Tovah? What's up with you? I got to get you out the house and show you a good time!"

I laughed and said, "Yeah, oh really?"

He said, "Yup, I sure am." He then asked me what I was doing tomorrow and I told him I had class in the evening. He asked me if he could take me out to lunch or an early dinner before class and I told him yes and we made plans to go to lunch so we could hang for a little while before class and then we hung up. I had thought about giving him my mom's address but I realized that his cousin Kori already knew where I lived so it was no point.

I turned over on my back staring up at the ceiling and was smiling ear to ear. I had this feeling in my stomach, I think it was butterflies. I have never felt this way- ever- about a guy. Just then I jumped up and went to my closet. Shit I thought, what am I going to wear?! Luckily, I have a lot to choose from but I don't want to be too overdressed because I still got to go to class afterwards. I got a lot of cute shit I been wanting to wear though. I should wear the Milano bodysuit he bought- naw that's a negative. I am not about to be wearing any bootie shorts to class. Shit the professor wouldn't probably let me in anyway. I know exactly what to wear. I'm not going to overdo it either. I bought two pairs of BoogaSuga jeans that I haven't rocked yet so I think I'll put the boyfriend jeans on tomorrow rather than the very rear jawns. I don't need my ass out for him or for my classmates. The boyfriend jeans were so comfortable when I tried them on and they just got that effortless cool look when you pair it with basically whatever. And, I'm going to pair it with these cute yellow flats I got from Saks-on sale of course and the shirt I bought at the same time. Since I only have that one class tomorrow, I can carry one of my designer bags, it's been a while since I carried one. Usually I would just carry a backpack or have on something small like a belt bag or fanny pack as Manda would say. Now that my outfit was taken care of I could concentrate on something else- my stomach- I was hungry.

I went back out to an empty living room. I guess Manda had gotten lucky because her door was closed. That's the only time she closed her door when she had company. Shit, it's been damn near two years since I got lucky. But maybe, just maybe my luck was starting to change.

I basically spent the rest of the night replaying my conversation with Haasan and fell asleep with my textbook open even though I never looked at it.

I pulled up in front of my spot and saw Kayla's Honda out front. That's my homie Quaan's girl. I didn't feel like running into her today- she can be a bit much sometimes. She comes off as bougie but her ratchet side comes out more often than not. I just wasn't in the mood for her tonight so I figured I'd give the lil shorty Tovah a call back. I wasn't expecting to hear from her so soon, I thought she was gonna be a stuck up jawn who either waited to call or wouldn't even bother.

Tovah turned out to be cool as hell and had a head on her shoulders. Going to college to be a nurse and shit that's what's up. We bussed it up for a minute and she told me that her Pops died a few years ago. That's fucked up, she still sound pretty hurt just saying it. Probably is, she said she was a daddy's girl. I know I'd be fucked up if something happened to my mom or my dad. But I'm a momma's boy and proud of it. I kept the conversation mostly light on my end. I did lie though about Sheena. I told her that we had broken up because of the long distance. I mean it is kind of true. We did break up for a quick minute because I wasn't feeling doing no long distance shit. But, she's only in Atlanta and when I realized how easy it was and actually an advantage for me, I quickly changed my mind and she was with it. So at least once a month I hop on a flight and stay down there with her for a few days. The tickets cheap as hell so that's a plus. It's been working for us for a while now. She hasn't even been back up here since we graduated. Her dad up and moved her and her younger sister to Georgia to be closer to his family since her mom passed away, so it's really no need for her to come up. Her mom had suffered from cancer throughout our entire time in high school and passed away the summer before senior year. It's still hard for her and even though I hate that she's there and I'm here, I still try to be there for her as much as I can. And since we not official for real, I still do me from time to time.

And Tovah little pretty ass, yeah...I'm definitely gonna do me and her.

That next day I woke up to the smell of turkey bacon calling me. I laid there in the bed for a few minutes trying to get myself together. I fought the urge to get up because I had to get my homework done before tonight. I had all day but I knew I would be too focused on was my lunch date with Haasan. And, I still had to fill Manda in on the details from last night and I'm pretty sure she had an earful for me too.

I went to the bathroom to put some water on my face and to brush my teeth. When I got back there was a turkey bacon, egg and cheese sandwich on the table next to my bed and a glass of orange juice. I picked up the sandwich, took a bite as I walked out of my bedroom to thank Manda.

"Oh, how I love thee, let me count the ways" I said to a smiling Manda. She was sitting in her favorite chair in the living room puffing on a joint.

After she exhaled through her nose she said, "You know I got you cousin...wit ya greedy ass."

"Whatever. How was your night? I'm surprised that you out here alone. I saw your door closed last night."

"Yeah, it was alright, Kori said she had to be to work early, inventory or some shit, I don't know."

"Uhm somebody don't sound too happy? What happened?"

"Nothing, naw, she alright, I don't know, we'll see. But what up with da bol, her cousin, what's his name?"

"Oh you mean Haasan? Yeah, we meeting up later on for lunch", I said nonchalantly.

"Okay, look at you! Bout time, it's been a minute since you hooked up."

"Excuse you, who said anything about hooking up? We going to get some food and that's that."

"You know what I meant, he's a potential hook up and there haven't been any as far as I can remember."

"Yeah, he got potential, I'll guess we'll see how it goes. Alright, let me get back to this work."

"Aiight cuzzo, damn you mirked that sandwich!"

"Shut up", I said while walking away and laughing.

After about an hour and a half I had finished the classwork that was due tonight and actually finished an assignment from one of my other classes that wasn't due until next week. I was feeling productive, I really think I was trying to keep myself busy from overthinking. I don't know, I was kind of anxious about my lunch date and I don't know why. Haasan had texted me a little while ago asking what time I'd be ready and I told him two-thirty which was now only a little over an hour away.

It was two-thirty five and I was dressed, looking cute and ready to go and Haasan called saying he was stuck in traffic and would be here a few minutes late. One thing I can't stand is tardiness. I can't stand waiting on people and today I was particularly irritated because I was hungry. Last thing, I want him to hear is my dang stomach growling. Luckily for me, he didn't take too long, he arrived at two forty-five. He texted me that he was outside and I came out to the car. He rolled down the window but didn't even get out the car to greet me or open the door for me. It was cool, but I took note. He was more handsome than I remembered, I think because he looked a little less thuggish than yesterday. Nothing is wrong with thuggish at all, but today he had on an Adidas sweat suit and he looked cute as hell.

He said, "Hey Tovah, nice to see you again and my bad, it must've been an accident or something because the e-way was backed up. You ready to eat?"

"Hi Haasan, yes I am and it's cool."

"I got just the place for us to go to. The food good, I went there once or twice before."

"Yeah, what's it called?"

"Pretty Girls Cook, you ever been?."

"Yeah, I heard of it and been wanted to come here. I always hear good things about it. Oh, that's what's up. I can't wait to see what the hype is all about."

"Oh yeah, word? I think you gon like it."

"We shall see."

The restaurant was out North so I was a little skeptical, which is one of the reasons I had never gone. But when we pulled up I was pleasantly surprised with the location, it wasn't bad at all. When we walked in I was impressed by the set-up, the décor was nice. There was a young girl who I guess was the hostess who seated us and gave us our menus. It was a lot of good choices and I really wanted the grilled cheese short rib sandwich but I didn't get it for two reasons. One because I was trying to be cute and I didn't want to fuck that sandwich up in front of Haasan-that wouldn't have been cute at all. The other because I still had to go to class later and when I asked, the waitress said that jawn was kind of hefty. I probably would have had the itis after. So, I went with a salmon salad and that jawn banged! It looked all pretty when it came out and the size of the salmon was bigger than what I had expected. Haasan got the grilled cheese short rib sandwich and I knew that I was going to make it my business to get that the next time. Not getting the sandwich was a good decision too, ain't no way I was gonna remain ladylike eating that big ass sandwich. On a second date maybe, not the first.

We conversed while we waited for our food. Haasan kind of eluded to what he's been doing since he graduated from high school. He said he had gone to CCP but realized quickly that school was not for him. My guess is that he was a street pharmacist although he never confirmed nor denied it, I mean I never outright asked. His words if I remember correctly were 'I got a couple hustles, I'm gonna get money one way or another. Being broke ain't never been me'.

I guess he was just as hungry as me because little was said during eating our meals. We was too busy fucking our food up. While we ate I recognized a familiar face walking in the door and began to smile. "What you smiling at?" Haasan asked. Before I could answer him, the guy and the girl came walking up to our table smiling also. "Damn, long time no see Tovah!" the guy said.

"Whiteboy what is up, I replied excitedly. I got up to hug him and said to the girl while kind of in a group hug, "It's seems like forever since I've seen y'all! Oh, I'm sorry, this is Haasan", extending my hand towards him. "Haasan, these are my friends Whiteboy and Nelly." Haasan said, "Whiteboy?" The three of us laughed. The girl whose name is Shanell but goes by Nelly spoke up and said, "Tov has been calling him that since ninth grade."

"Yeah, it's been so long, what is your real name?" I said jokingly.

Gerry finally spoke up and extended his hand to Haasan, "It's Gerry and nice to meet you Haasan."

"Gerry, yeah, you too. Oh y'all go way back?"

"Yup, I spent a lot of time throughout high school with these two. And, what? I haven't seen y'all since? Dang, I don't even remember." The hostess who had been standing nearby the entire time, interrupted our brief reunion and in a nice way told them it was time to go to their table. "Go ahead y'all, I'll stop by before we leave."

I sat back down smiling and got right back into my salad. Haasan didn't seem to be too pleased judging by the look on his face. "Everything okay?" I asked him.

"Yeah, besides you being a little rude, I'm cool."

"Excuse me?" I swallowed my food and said, "How was I rude?"

"Getting up hugging niggas and shit. You don't think that was rude?"

"Those are my friends, really good friends that I haven't seen in a while. No, I don't think it was rude at all."

"You got me looking all crazy."

"What are you talking about, how do I have you looking crazy?"

"Forget it."

"Yeah, let's." I was irked as hell. I just met this dude and he already showing signs of jealousy, at least that's what I think it was. The waitress came back over and asked if we needed anything. I looked over at Haasan and said "Check?"

He agreed and repeated, "yeah, just the check, thanks."

I excused myself and went over to say goodbye to Whiteboy and Nelly. We exchanged numbers and promised to be in touch soon. I met Haasan over by the register where he was getting his change from the cashier. He went over and tipped the waitress and then we were out the door. When we got to the car he opened the door for me this time. Once he got in, we were both quiet for a minute and he looked over at me and said, "Look, I'm sorry. I got an image to maintain and I wasn't trying to—

I interrupted him, "an image? Oh, did you know somebody in there?"

"No, but still."

"Still what? Haasan I just met you. This was our first time out. I'm not your girl, you're not my man and it seems more like you were jealous than anything."

"Jealous, the fuck I gotta be jealous about?"

"Exactly. There was nothing to be jealous about but the fact that you said that I was 'getting up hugging niggas and shit' makes me believe you were jealous over nothing. Whiteboy and I are friends and the fact that I am explaining *this to someone I just met—on our first date at that isn't a good sign."*

"Look, I'm sorry. I guess I can be a little jealous sometimes, everybody can."

"Yeah, they can but that was something small, I don't wanna imagine how you'd act about something a little bit bigger."

"I hope this don't change your view of me Tovah."

"Haasan, I'm just forming an opinion about you, that's what this lunch date was about. For us to get to know one another better. You showed a red flag and one thing my mom always told me was to never ignore the red flags."

"I think you making it bigger than what it is. It's not that serious."

"I'm not making anything bigger than what it is, I'm speaking facts. And a fact is that I have male friends, a lot of them. I might not see them or talk to them all the time like I

did back in high school but they're still my friends. And if and when I run into them no matter who I'm with, I'm going to show the same love I always have."

"That goes both ways. How would you feel if a female came in and I got up to hug her or something?"

"Haasan, it doesn't matter to me. We literally just met. The only time I could or would feel some type of way is if you hugging and grinding on her on some inappropriate shit. You were wrong to call me rude because I was happy to see two of my friends and greeted them in a way I would if I were with anyone."

"You right, I'm sorry. You accept my apology?"

"Uhm hmm, I accept it."

"Damn. It don't sound like it."

"I do accept your apology. I can still be a little irked at the same time too."

He laughed, "You right. Well, let's get you back to being alright. You still got some time to waste before class, you want to spend a little more time with me so I can make it up to you or you tryna get away from me as fast as you can?"

"Well, since you apologized...what you got in mind?"

"Since it's nice out, how about we go over to the park and sit and talk?"

"That sounds okay."

"Good, he smiled, I'm trying sway you back to liking me again."

"Who said I ever liked you?" I said sarcastically.

"Damn", he laughed, that's cold. You gon make me work, huh?"

"Yup", I said giving a little smirk.

"I guess I deserve it. I can't help it though. Look at you. I can't see no dude just tryna be friends with you. Shorty, you gorgeous."

Blushing, I said, "Flattery will get you everywhere."

"I thought that a work. At least I finally got a smile from you."

Haasan parked up on Kelly Drive and instead of getting out the car we just sat inside and talked until it was time me for me to get to class. He was outside after class to pick me up which wasn't planned. He said that I shouldn't have to call a cab or whatever I had planned on doing since he had dropped me off. I thought that was kind of nice of him and we sort of just started hanging out a lot after that. He turned out to be really cool and was intent on showering me with gifts. I hadn't seen any more signs to warn me away so I kind of went with the flow with him. It's funny though, we never really talked about us being a couple we just sort of became one. Even when we had sex for the first time, it just sort of happened. I think the first time we talked about our relationship status was about two years in and my period was late and it was possible that I could be pregnant. When I told him he made a comment suggesting that I keep the pregnancy. I remember talking about terminating it and I said something like 'we're not even in a real relationship so why would I'. Honestly though, I wouldn't have even considered keeping a baby. I had a plan for my life and I was determined to carry it out and a baby did not fit into those plans at all.

He asked what the big deal about being official was. I hit him with the 'you don't think I've heard shit about you in the streets? I let it go—because technically you're not my man. And, if you ever hear shit about me, give me that same respect'. You saw it all in his face, jaws clenched up and everything-he ain't like that. Yeah, it was kind of petty on my part, but I figured that he needed to know that it go both ways- that he couldn't come at me about anything that he might hear. Only thing, I wasn't doing shit, I wasn't entertaining nobody before I met him and didn't plan on it then. I liked what we had but he basically was having his cake and eating it too.

After that comment and the pregnancy scare, which thankfully was just a scare, we became official and more careful. I started taking birth control pills faithfully and Haasan continued wearing condoms for a while, but I couldn't tell you the last time he wore one.

Once we became official our relationship seemed to get better, it was good and I was happy, but lately not so much. We have our ups and downs but doesn't everybody? He goes out of town more than he used to and I'm not sure I believe him when he says it's to go upstate to visit his brother. I still love him and all it just seems that we are growing apart and are just in this relationship that's going nowhere. I have tried to talk to him about the future of our relationship and he brushes me off saying stuff like 'we're good' or 'what we've got is good'. All good things must come to an end and the way I've been feeling lately...that will be sooner than later.

It was 7:20 when I got to Longhorn's parking lot and to my surprise Sallahdeen was already parked in a black F-150. It wasn't exactly what I expected him to be driving but then again I don't know what I was expecting. It was a nice truck though. He was on the phone when I pulled in next to him, but he smiled showing those pretty ass teeth of his to let me know that he saw me. As I got out of my car, he was getting out of his too. He had hung up the phone and walked around the truck and greeted me with a hug.

"Hello Miss Tovah, nice to see you again and on time", he smiled and step backed while looking at the watch on his wrist.

I said, *"Hello Sallahdeen, nice to see you too and same. You look nice."* I meant it, he had on a tan shirt that hugged his pecks and showcased what I could only imagine was a six-pack underneath. He paired it with a pair of brown pants and tan and brown shoes. He looked good as hell and I tried my best not to stare. I was happy with the outfit that I chose to wear. I had on white high waisted pants that hugged my ass and a matching sleeveless halter top with a pair white and silver heels. He walked me around the passenger side of the truck, opened the door and helped me climb into the truck. I said to him, *"you're quiet, everything alright?"*

He said, *"Yes, everything is good. I'm taking you all in, you look even more beautiful than when I saw you earlier."*

I blushed a little and said, *"Thank you."* He made sure I was in and went around and got in the driver's seat. He looked at me and smiled and pulled out of the parking lot. I asked him, *"So where are we going?"*

He answered, *"To go get some food."*

"Ha,ha I know that but where to?"

"You'll see when we get there."

"I hope you chose somewhere good, I haven't eaten since earlier."

"Oh, yeah? This place I'm taking you to has some good food, their seafood is bomb too. I know the dude who owns it. It's a nice spot out the way, I think you'll like it."

"You think so, huh?"

He said, *"Yeah, I do. So, what's up Miss Tovah?"*

Before I could answer, my phone rang and Haasan's face popped up on the screen. I muted it. I didn't want to send it to voicemail because then he would call right back.

Sallahdeen looked at me, smiled and said, *"Oh, ya man checking for you already? I don't blame him."*

"You don't blame him?"

"Naw, look at you. If I had a girl as fine as you, I'd be on her top too."

Haasan was calling again. Sallahdeen said, *"Tov, you mind as well answer the phone and say something because he's not gonna stop calling."*

I turned to him and smiled and said, *"Tov?"*

He said, *"you gonna tell me that nobody don't call you Tov?"*

I said, *"Yeah, people I'm cool with and that know me".*

He said, *"Well, I plan on getting to know you and I must be cool because you agreed to go to dinner with me."*

I answered, *"You aiight"* We both laughed.

He said, *"I'll take that.* He began to mess around with the radio, *"what kind of music you listen to?"*

"Old school for real, you don't know nothing about that. And I'm talking old school everything- rap, R&B, whatever."

"What?!" He then picked up his phone and went through his music. He seemed happy with his choice and said, *"shiiit, what you know about this?"* Tony! Toni! Toné! *Whatever you Want* began to play.

I smiled, *"Oh you got lucky with that one. That's my jawn for real."*

"Uhn, huh, I told you."

That's how we spent the rest of the drive, talking about music. The place he was taking me to was a little bit out the way so we got a few picks in. Sallahdeen was cool as hell, it felt like I've been known him and not that I just met him earlier today. I still can't believe I'm on a date with somebody else.

We finally arrived at our destination and pulled into the parking lot of the restaurant when Haasan called back. Sallahdeen got out the truck and I finally answered the phone. *"Damn, Tov, what the hell?"*

I said, *"Hello to you too Haasan"*.

He said, *"You've been MIA all day"* and I shot back, *"LIES. I called you earlier a couple of times and once you called me by mistake and I called you right back and you didn't answer."*

He said, *"I was taking care of business and you know how shit slips my mind. But anyway, where you at, what's up, isn't today your day off?"*

I rolled my eyes at the phone and said, *"my day off is damn near over. I was trying to connect with you earlier to see what we was doing. I'm out with a couple of friends from school, we decided to go out for some drinks"*. Lying to him was easier than I thought it would be.

He said, *"aiight where y'all at, I'll come through"*.

I said *"nope, it's cool. I'm hanging out with them tonight. I'll holla later"* and then hung up the phone.

"Hello." I looked at my phone. *I know she didn't just hang up on me. Yo, she been talking real slick lately.*

"Yo, what she hung up on you?" Raoul asked laughing. *"She tired of ya shit man."*

"Man, fuck you talking bout? Mind ya business any fucking way."

"I keep telling you. My girl come at me with the same shit, 'You don't spend enough time, you always out in them streets, yada, yada, yada…' Tovah been putting up with ya shit for so long man. Between Sheena and the shit she hear out here in the streets…man, I'm just saying these females worse than us when it comes to cheating and shit. They sneaky as hell too."

"Man Raoul, Tovah ain't going nowhere and ain't doin' shit. And she never even had a clue about Sheena and that shit over anyway. Just because Jess was out here fucking

Tom, Dick and Lenny", I started laughing. *Raoul had found out his girl was cheating on him with some bol Lenny from out North. It's crazy how he found out though. Lenny's baby mom, who just so happens to be Raoul's cousin, came home and found them fucking in their bed. Raoul's cousin Niecey fucked up his girl and the bol Lenny. That shit still fucks with Raoul because he was in love like a motherfucker with Jess. He would've probably took her back but because everybody know about what happened he knew he'd look like a nutass dude. And, his cousin went to jail over that shit, she stabbed Lenny up pretty bad. Word out that he gotta wear a colostomy bag. He didn't press charges either but commonwealth picked that shit up.*

Raoul was heated, like always when anybody brought Jess up. *"You can keep laughing, these bitches keep secrets better than you think. Trust me, I got three sisters and they be in whole other fucking relationships and their niggas be clueless. Don't be knowing shit."*

"Yeah, that's them. I know Tovah though. She love me and besides she don't have enough time in the day to be fucking with anybody else. Between me and her job, I'm not worried about shit."

Raoul added, *"Yeah, if you say so."*

"Yeah I say so." I know I ain't been the most faithful boyfriend to Tovah but…man fuck that Raoul ain't getting in my head. I know my baby, she a good girl. She got eyes for me and for me only.

The evening with Sallahdeen was filled with lots of conversation and a lot of laughing. The conversation flowed effortlessly and we conversed for hours about any and everything. I was smitten and it seemed he was too.

I hadn't smiled or enjoyed myself this much as a result of a man in some time. I don't remember it ever being like this with Haasan. We continued to talk. At one point he revealed he had a crush from the time he saw me in the parking lot. He laughed and said it was fate that brought us both to Longhorn's. I wasn't fazed. My confidence spoke to me that of course he would have a crush, who wouldn't. At the same time I wasn't sure I believed him. After all, that's how the game is sometimes played, right? But, it was kind of weird that we wound up at Longhorn's at the same time just a few minutes later. Maybe fate, maybe just coincidence.

As the days went on our conversations increased. Then came the visit. As I sat on the step of my mom's house and waited for him to arrive, I wondered if the strong attraction I felt over the phone would be present when I finally saw him again in person. He turned the corner and saw me sitting there and smiled. I then smiled back. I still don't know what to make of this. How I could feel this way about someone in so little time had me a little confused. He got out of the truck and gave me a hug and I welcomed his embrace. I loved how he smelled and it felt so good, it felt so right to be in his arms. The attraction was so intense. It felt like you could see my heart beating out of my chest.

He released me from his arms and smiled at me, *"Finally, I get to see you again."*

I couldn't stop smiling, *"I don't know why, but I had butterflies in my stomach all day. I couldn't wait to see you".*

"That's good to know."

"It's good to know that I had butterflies or that I couldn't wait to see you?"

"Both, he said while laughing, *I felt like you were selling me dreams. I wasn't sure I was gonna ever see you in person again."*

"Selling you dreams? I like that. But you know it wasn't on purpose. I got a lot going on with work—and you know, my boyfriend."

"I know, I know. We gotta fix that problem."

"I thought we were going to leave that topic alone?"

"Aiight, you right. But are we going to stand out here or you gon invite me in?"

I took his hand and walked him up the steps and into the house. While we were on the phone last night, I casually mentioned that I was going to my mom's house to feed her two cats after I was done my shift. She was going to be away for the next two weeks so I was given the task of feeding her '*fur babies*' as she calls them, while she was gone. She goes to visit her brother- my uncle, usually twice a year. He and his family has lived in Florida for the past twentysomething years.

Sallahdeen looked around the house as he entered and seemed to like what he was seeing. *"Yo, your mom's house is nice as hell. I always liked how split levels homes are set up. This the type of home I always wanted when I finally get my own."*

"Yeah, I like it." Sallahdeen had just gotten here but I was already over the small talk. I had been waiting to see him since the last time we were together and I just wanted to kiss him.

"Is this the house you lived in growing up?" he asked.

"Yup, me, my mom and dad."

"Tov, are you cool? You seem to be, I don't know…"

"Actually, I'm not Sallahdeen."

"What's wrong?" He asked.

"You've been here with me for damn near ten minutes and you still haven't kissed me."

He broke out into a big ass smile and said, *"Say less."* He then bent down and lifted my chin up towards him and sort of cradled my face with one hand and put his soft lips on mine. He proceeded to slip his tongue in my mouth and circling around mine and ended the kiss by sort of playfully licking my lips before kissing them again softly. To say that was the most perfect kiss I had ever experienced in my life would not be an exaggeration. I was somewhat taken aback after the kiss, it felt like a dream. I guess it took me a few seconds to get over that kiss because when I opened my eyes Sallahdeen was looking at me smiling.

I smiled and said, *"What are you smiling at?"*

He answered still smiling, *"You. I told you before I was a good kisser"*.

"You aiight." We both bust out laughing. If only he knew how much I wanted him inside me right now. *"Now, what were you talking about before?"*

"I believe I was telling you how dope I think you are."

"Uh, no you weren't, but I'm listening."

"Miss Tovah are you blushing?"

"Maybe."

Sallahdeen pulled me close to him and I tried to hide my face in his chest and he said, *"Tov, you know how long I've been waiting to see that pretty face of yours again, c'mon look at me."*

I looked up at him and he had this kind of serious look on his face. I could feel his heart beating against mine. He said, *"I'm going to make it my mission to make you mine.*

I've never felt this way about anyone in my life. I know you feel it. He smiled. *I probably sound crazy, we've only known each other for what? Not even two whole weeks but, I don't know...I just know I want you all to myself."*

"What am I supposed to say to that Sallahdeen?"

"Nothing. I didn't ask you a question. I was just stating facts, that's all. And I wanted you to know how I feel from the rip so there isn't any confusion."

"Oh okay, but what kind of confusion you talking about?"

"You can't ever say that I wasn't clear about what I wanted. You are what I want and if you're happy with your current situation and don't see that changing any time soon then I mind as well go. Is that what you want?"

I slightly pulled from his embrace unable to look at him and said, *"No, but..."* I didn't know what to say.

Sallahdeen let me go and kissed me on the cheek. *"Tov, it was really good seeing you. When you able to finish that sentence, holla at me."*

"You're leaving? You just got here", I said.

"Yeah, I'm a go." And he left.

Left me standing in the middle of the living room stuck. After talking on the phone for hours the past two weeks, I get ten minutes, a bangin' ass kiss and what felt like an ultimatum! I thought the side chicks usually give the ultimatums not the other way around. I had to laugh out loud at the last thought. *"The fuck?!"*

I locked up my mom's house and drove home. The entire drive I couldn't help but to think about Sallahdeen. Is this some sort of game he playing? Trying to play hard to get or something. Like really? My stomach hurt when the thought of not seeing him anymore came to mind. Yeah, that definitely wasn't happening. And, leaving Haasan alone wasn't happening either, the thought had never even crossed my mind until I met Sallahdeen.

I thought getting in the game was going to be fun, but I'm quickly learning it's not that fun and it damn sure ain't a game.

I walked in the house and saw the light from the tv on. Uncle George had fell asleep on the couch again. I tried to be quiet but I guess he had heard me. I don't know why I didn't use the back entrance anyway.

"Hey nephew, what's going on?"

"Nothing, bouta get like you and take it down."

"Naw, I was watching—"

"Yeah, aiight, the tv was watching you."

"Man, I can't even lie, I sat down and turned on the tv and it was over", he laughed, then stood up stretching. *"I'm surprised your aunt didn't come down and tell me to come upstairs."*

"She probably up there sleeping herself. But, I'm finna take a shower and relax. I had a long day. Aiight Unc, 'night."

"Alright Deen, you good?"

"Yeah, I'm good."

"Okay, goodnight."

I made my way downstairs to the basement. I been living with my aunt and uncle for the past year and a half since my parents were killed in a car accident. Head on collision with a drunk driver. It's been a big adjustment. Not that I'm living with them because they cool as shit. But, the move from Atlanta. I mean, it was my decision so I'm not complaining. My aunt and uncle didn't really want me to be down Atlanta by myself-at least not right after. It wasn't like I was by myself for real, I had some family in Marietta. They were older though and I wasn't as close with them as I was with my Aunt Toni and Uncle George. Aunt Toni is my mom's only sister and we used to come up to Philly to visit and she came down to see us a lot so we're pretty tight. My uncle is a long-haul truck driver so he's always on the road and Aunt Toni never liked being away from her big sis for too long. She didn't work and they didn't have any kids so it was easy for her to pick up and come down to visit whenever her husband was on the road. My mom always used to say Aunt Toni found her perfect man because growing up she always got bored with her boyfriends real quick. I knew Aunt Toni loved Uncle George but she damn sure laughed and didn't deny it when my mom said it to her.

It's alright living up here, I have my own space and they give me space. Uncle George started doing more local drives so he's home more often than he used to be. I think he wanted to be close to home for Aunt Toni and maybe even for me. I don't mind and it seems like Aunt Toni likes that he is home more too. She didn't take losing my mom too well. I think it helped both of us to be with each other after they were killed. I don't think I would have wanted to stay in Atlanta without my parents though, we were really close. Even though it's been more than a year I still can't believe that they're both gone.

Philly is just different, it has a different vibe and I haven't been feeling it…until now. Since I met Tovah, man, I don't know. That girl is the truth. She's everything that I always wanted in a female and she reminds me so much of my mom it's crazy. I know if moms or pops would have met her they would've loved her. It's just one obstacle with her and I don't know if it's going to be an easy one to get pass…but she's worth it so I'm definitely going to try. Time will tell how this plays out.

I don't know what I'm trying to get into tonight. Qua and Mir said they was trying to hit up the new strip club but I don't know, my phone been blowing up the past few days. I put all my jawns on the back burner because I was chillin with this lil' Puerto Rican shorty but that was getting old because I see her being clingy. Even Kori been on my top again lately. We always been on and off, but I knew from the beginning something was off. She's not gay, she calls herself bi which is fine with me, she just had a man that she forgot to mention. It probably wouldn't have mattered, I would have still fucked her but when I was eating her shit that first night she was going crazy and begged for the dick. Shorty forgot who the fuck she was with. I asked her was she ready for the strap-on and she tried to play it off and clammed up a little. I asked her straight out was she gay or bi or whatever and she admitted that she guess she was bi. She fucked with females from time to time but she had a man and he didn't have a clue about her extracurricular dealings. She said that she was attracted to females and males and let me know that she loves to eat pussy too if I was ever interested. I told her I'm cool, I'll pass on that.

Tovah came walking in the door, *"what's up Tov?"*

"Hey Manda, what you up to?"

"Trying to figure out what I'm getting into. Where you coming from, auntie's?"

"Yeah. I need a night out, why don't we hang out tonight, it's been a while?"

"Oh shit, what then happened? You for real? Whatchu trying to do party or bullshit?"

"Not trying to party, I just need a drink or two to clear my damn mind."

"Okay, then where you tryna go?"

"Shit, you Miss party-all-the-time, take me to one of the spots you hang out. A chill spot though where we can get

something to eat. I didn't eat nothing but a corn muffin today and that was this morning."

"How bout Carlette's, the spot I told you about with the crab fries? That's a chill spot for real."

"Sound like a plan. I hope them jawns bang the way you be talking about 'em."

"Cuz, I know what you like, trust they bang. And their wings not bad either."

"Alright, cool. Carlette's it is. Round what time? Seven, eight?"

"It's up to you, but I think the kitchen open at seven so that's a good time."

"Ard, I'm going to my room and relax for a little bit."

"Cousin, you cool?"

"Naw, but I will be. We'll talk, I just need to shower and change."

"Don't be trying to get cute unless you want one of them old heads up in there."

She laughed while walking away and said, *"Please, I'm always cute!"*

My phone went off, I looked at it and saw it was a text from Kori saying she miss me and could I make some time for her tonight. She must be going through it with whatever nigga she fucking now because it seems like that's the only time she be on my top. I responded to her text with 'how bout tonight?' She was down, I told her around midnight because I already had plans. She was cool with it. It's been a while since I hooked up with her and couldn't wait to put my lips on her lips. She tastes so fucking good and I loved sucking all over her body. Shit I was getting myself excited. I knew for sure that if I had a dick it would be hard as a rock right now. And since she down with the strap, I'm definitely gon fuck the shit out of her later.

It's been a while since me and Manda hung out solo and it was just what I needed. Carlette's turned out to be a real chill spot. It's more like a neighborhood bar but not one that you feel a little I don't know- eerie about going in. Manda ain't never lied about it being mostly old heads either, that's probably why it's so chill. And them damn crab fries was the truth! She always finding some place to hang out. One thing for sure though, no matter where you go, you always run into at least one person you know. And tonight, it was Sallahdeen's corny ass friend, whose name I found out was Sam. Figures he would be here, he fit in with the rest of the old heads with the clothes he be wearing. I didn't even see him, he spotted me. Me and Manda were playing a game of pool and one of the bartenders or waitress or whoever she was brought two glasses of Courvoisier to us and pointed him out. When I looked over he raised his glass to us.

"The fuck is that?" Manda asked.

"That's Sam, Sallahdeen's 'homie'".

Manda looked back at him and nodded her head with the glass raised in her hand to thank him. He nodded back at her. *"So what should we toast to?"* She asked.

I answered, *"Let's toast to us. Family."* She nodded in agreement. We raised our glasses, palms underneath the bottoms, clinked and each took a sip. We both made faces, I never was a big fan of any kind of cognac and Manda rarely drank, she was a smoker but every once in a while if the occasion called for it, she'd drink. She said she didn't like the feeling that alcohol and weed together gave her. Me, I was more of a wine drinker and if I did drink something heavy, it definitely had to be fruity or mixed with something. Shots has never been my thing, I can't handle it.

"So you gon tell me what's going on? Something is obviously wrong?" Manda finally asked.

"Men trouble." I said.

Manda laughed then looked at me while lining up her next shot. *"Men trouble? Ahhh, you funny."*

"What's so funny? I am having men problems."

"Alright, alright my bad. What's the problem Tov?"

"Well, you know I've been seeing the guy Sallahdeen for a few weeks, right?" I asked.

"Yeah…"

"Well, I think I'm falling for him," I admitted.

"Okay…and what's wrong with that?"

"Manda, have you forgotten about Haasan- my boyfriend?" I asked her.

"Cousin you already know how I feel about that situation. You not even happy with him, y'all shit been over a long time ago. Y'all really just fucking partners and y'all barely do that."

"Well damn."

"Naw for real, you say it all the time and don't do shit about it. Shit, I was glad when you called yourself 'getting back in the game'."

"Yeah, I'm in it and playing the game is not as easy as I thought was going to be."

She asked, *"What were you expecting though? You ain't never been a playa like me-"*

"Oh God, here we go", I said as I rolled my eyes.

"No for real, I'm just saying, you got in the game because you're so-called over Haasan's BS, now you then found somebody that you like so what's the problem? What he don't like you or something?"

"Of course he likes me."

Manda laughed, *"Yeah, of course. Then now it's time to end—wait let me use your line—'this relationship or whatever you wanna call it that's going nowhere'."*

"Easier said than done."

"You holding on to what y'all had not what y'all have, because for real for real what do y'all got now?"

"Damn, you tryna to kick knowledge and shit…when you put it like that, shaking my head, I continued…*it's still easier said than done."*

We finished the night after another round or two of drinks and another game of pool-this time between Manda and an oldhead who had next. Neither Sallahdeen nor Haasan was on my mind for the time being and their names wasn't mentioned again. A night out was exactly what I needed.

We pulled up in front of our apartment and saw Kori's car parked out front. *"Damn, stalker much?"* I laughed.

"Chill, I texted her that I was on my way home and told her to be on her way."

"Oh, because I was about to say what if it wasn't me that you pulled up with."

"Trust, I got this. And for real Tov, what you got isn't really a problem. You know what you have to do."

"And what's that?"

"Whatever makes you happy."

I wasn't expecting that answer, but she was right. *"Thanks cousin, I love you."*

"I know, I love you too."

We got out of the car and Manda walked over to Kori who was now leaning on her car. I waved over to her and kept it moving. Soon as I got in the door, I went straight to my bedroom, closed the door and came straight out of my clothes. I went in the bathroom to wash my face and to brush my teeth, showering would have to wait until morning. I was feeling tipsy and wanted to keep that feeling. I put my phone on the charger and climbed into bed.

I tried to sleep but I couldn't. Haasan had called me but I ignored his call. I actually watched it ring but wasn't up to talking to him. He texted me after and said 'I guess you're sleep'. Haasan trusts me so much that's why it is so easy to start seeing someone else. I mean, why wouldn't he? I never gave him any reason to think or suspect that I would ever cheat. But he on the other hand…I don't know. I know he's no angel but right now I'm just looking for reasons to excuse the fact that I am falling for someone else. All I could picture was Sallahdeen walking out the door. My heart sank every time I thought about the 'situation' that I have put myself in.

My phone lit up again. This time it was a text from Sallahdeen. I opened it up and it was an emoji seeing if I was asleep. I answered 'no'. He texted back asking if it was okay for him to call. I didn't reply back, I just called him. He answered on the first ring and said, *"Hey beautiful."*

"Hey Sallahdeen." I called myself playing it all cool but I was so happy to hear his voice.

"I'm surprised you're still up, I thought you were an early bird."

"I know right? But, I actually just got in not too long ago."

"Oh for real?"

"Yeah, I was-"

"No, you don't have to- I was just-"

I interrupted him, *"Excuse me, like I was saying I was out with my cousin, we went out to get a few drinks."*

"That's what's up. Y'all have fun?" He asked.

"Fun? I don't know about that but I did enjoy myself. I needed to get out. Oh and I saw your homie, Sam. He bought us a drink."

"Oh y'all was at Carlette's then?" He asked laughing.

"I'm guessing that's his spot?"

"Yeah, he stay up in there. He took me there once, it was aiight. Them crab fries was bangin, but I'm cool on that spot."

"They do bang! They live up to the hype. I know what you mean. It's not somewhere that I would wanna hang at all the time. Why you cool on it though? Them old heads be coming at you?" I asked laughing.

"Yup, you called it! And why wouldn't they?"

I was cracking up, *"Here you go! But you right, why wouldn't they?"*

"Right, it's hard to look pass all this sexual chocolate."

Now we both were laughing. Out of the blue Sallahdeen said, *"Tovah, I'm sorry about earlier. I been waiting to see you for the last two weeks and then when I saw you I put all my shit out there on you. I didn't even plan on saying all that and now I don't the next time I'm going to see you…if you wanna even see me."*

"What you doing tomorrow?" I asked him.

"Huh?"

I repeated him, *"Huh? I said what are you doing tomorrow? I have to go back pass my mom's to feed her cats, how about you come by?"* That was a little white lie. I had fed the cats enough so I wouldn't have to go over there every day more like every other. But, I wanted to see him so one little lie won't hurt.

"Sounds like a plan."

I could hear the smile in his voice. *"It's a plan."* And I bet he could hear the smile in mine. *"Goodnight Sallahdeen."*

"Goodnight beautiful."

We hung up. It felt like a weight had been lifted off of me. I was so relieved that he reached out that I couldn't stop smiling. I laid in the bed and replayed our brief conversation. Tomorrow couldn't come soon enough.

I woke up to the sound of my phone ringing and saw that it was Haasan. *"Hello"*, I answered in my hoarse sleepy voice.

"Good morning babe, what you still doing sleep?" He said.

"My alarm should be bout to go off, why you up so early?"

"I just got in, I figured you'd be up so I called. Don't make plans for lunch today, I'm a come through and bring you something."

"Alright babe, let me get up and get myself together. I'll see you later."

"Alright, later", he said and then we both hung up.

I just sat there on the edge of the bed for a few seconds a little thankful that Haasan had called. I must've set my alarm to pm last night when I adjusted it trying to get a few extra minutes in. If he didn't call who knows how long I would've slept. Another thing I woke up thankful for is that I didn't have a damn hangover. I took it easy last night but I thought that Courvoisier was gonna be trouble for me this morning. Luckily for me, that wasn't the case. I finally got up and went in to the bathroom to shower and start my day.

My day at work was unlike any other day except that my mind was totally somewhere else…or maybe I should say on someone else. To be more specific it was on both Haasan and Sallahdeen. I haven't seen Haasan in two days but so much has happened in these two days that it seems longer. Two days ago I was perfectly fine around Haasan with no guilt at all that I had gone on a date with someone else and have also been communicating a lot with that someone else. Now, shit is just different. I have kissed Sallahdeen and am actually thinking about having sex with him. Who am I kidding? I am having sex with him-- today. Just thinking about it makes my pussy throb.

Anyway, Haasan is on his way. He texted if there was anything in particular that I wanted to eat and I just texted him *'not really, surprise me'*. He didn't even text back, I knew he was hot. He hates when I make him decide because then when I'm not satisfied with what he bought, I kind of play around with my food. I tell him to take me out to eat rather than always trying to chill and order takeout. His argument is for me to cook sometimes. I told him he got the wrong girl. I don't mind a night in at all, but damn a girl likes to get cute every once in a while and go out with her man. I wear scrubs all week and would like to let my hair down so to speak. Honestly, I can't remember the last time we had a real date night. I'm not counting the movies as a date because that's just something we do. We both consider ourselves movie buffs, me with horror movies and him all things action and especially comic book movies specifically the MCU. Haasan will go to the movies by himself or with his friends on opening night and by the time I go with him he more than likely already saw the movie. It kind of takes the fun out of it for me, knowing that he already saw it, so yeah that's why I don't consider going to the movies with him a real date.

I made my way down to the hospital cafeteria which was crowded as usual but I was able to get a table with no problem. I'm not even that hungry which is unusual for me because I can eat. I would have met him outside like I sometimes do but it was raining out and I didn't feel like going to my locker to get my jacket and umbrella that was doing too much. Anyway, he seemed like he was tryna see me and not do a drive-by. When he just dropping off, he'll let me know…this morning he said don't make any plans for lunch so the cafeteria it is. I texted him earlier to let him know what time I was going on my lunch break. I sat down and called him to see how much longer he was going to be. He picked up the phone saying, *"Right on time"* as I see him come walking in to the cafeteria.

"Oh hey, there you are", I said as I stood up and waved to him, he smiled when he saw me. He came over with two bags and placed them on the table and as I began to sit back down, he said, *"Damn, I don't get no love today?"*

"My bad babe, what was I thinking?" I said while half smiling and rolling my eyes at the same time.

"Yeah, I don't know. You know I need my hug when I see you baby", he said while embracing me. As he let me go, he asked *"How's your day going? Everything good?"*

"Yeah, everything's good, I'm a little tired though."

"Yeah, I see. You not even going through the bags like usual and I got one of your favorites".

"I see it. Thank you Haasan." I began taking the food out the bag. He had went to a restaurant in Chinatown and got my usual order of Chicken Katsu and Shrimp Tempura Sushi.

"Alright, what's up, what I do now?"

"What are you talking about?"

"You called me Haasan and you being all formal and shit."

"What? I laughed. *I'm being formal? What does that even mean?"*

"Yeah, the only time you really call me Haasan is when you upset about something. So again, what's wrong now?"

"Nothing is wrong. I told you, I'm just a little tired. Me and Manda hung out last night and I had a couple of drinks and I guess not enough sleep."

"Y'all hung out? You on a work night having drinks?" He asked.

Yeah, you sound surprised, is that a crime?"

"Naw, no crime smartass. I am a little surprised though. You've been hanging out a lot lately."

I laughed, *"Really? I been out twice lately and if you call that a lot I don't know what to say. I'm tired of just working and coming home. I've been on a regular schedule for a minute now and I need to get out more. Have some fun. You know what that is right?"*

"So what you tryna say?"

"Haasan, you already know. I'm not going to keep having this conversation with you. We don't spend no time together and if I gotta have fun without you that's exactly what I'm going to do."

"What does that mean?"

"What do you mean what do I mean? There's no hidden meaning. It can't get any clearer than what I said."

"Every time we see each other, it's the same conversation."

"Yeah because nothing changes and I'm getting sick of it. I know my schedule caused some issues between us before and I changed it so we could get back to how we was. But I've been back on mornings for how long now? Three months? And, nothing has changed. You know the streets talk, tell me the truth are you cheating on me?" I know I got some nerve but why not reverse the shit. It's a part of the game right?

"What, where the fuck that come from?! Talking about the streets be talking? You sound like Manda for real! Did she tell you something? Since when you got your ear to the streets?"

"NO Manda didn't tell me anything! You always avoid the real shit. And the real shit is that it don't feel like we're in a relationship any more, it seems like we're friends with benefits -and shit barely any benefits."

"Wow Tov! Is that how you really feel? Or somebody in your ear feeding you some bullshit?"

"You could think whatever you want but the fact is that I'm not happy with the way things are and you seem to be just fine with that. Lately, I find myself comparing our relationship to other people and realize we don't do shit. We've been together for damn near five years and never been away together and no A.C. don't count. It's sad and I'm too young for this. And, if you remember you were the one that used to tell me that you were going to show me how to live,

how to have fun and that I was too young not to be living.
What happened, what changed?"

Haasan sat there quiet and you could see he was fuming. I had hit him with the truth and he didn't say a word.

I asked him, *"So you're not going to say anything?"*

He leaned over kissed me on the cheek and said, *"We'll talk later. Enjoy your food, I'll holla at you."*

After he left, I sat at the table for a couple of minutes playing around with the food he had bought me. This was the second day in a row that a dude left me standing or sitting where I was feeling somewhat baffled. In the soap operas the woman usually walk or storms out on the man, why in this little soap opera I'm starring in is it the other way around? The thought just made me shake my head and sigh out loud. I put the food back in the bag and as I walked pass the trash bin I threw the bag in.

Tovah fucked me up with the shit she was talking. Shit, maybe Raoul was on to something. I don't think she cheating but she damn sure tired of my shit. She was talking real shit and it fucked me up cause I couldn't even say shit. I just sat there looking stupid. I gotta redeem myself because I felt like a damn fool. Shit, I still feel like a fool when I think about how I had to be looking. And she know it because I don't remember a time that I've ever been at a loss for words.

Ain't nothing stupid about me, Tovah is a good girl, she's a catch, I know this and she definitely knows. She got goals and plans for her future and I haven't come across too many females that seem to have all their shit figured out like she do. I gotta step up my game real rap. If I'm being truthful, I don't even deserve her but I'm gonna change. It ain't gonna happen overnight but what I know is that I'm not gonna be like them oldheads I be talking to always talking about the one that got away. Tovah ain't going nowhere and I'm a make sure of that.

I went about the rest of my day as usual but with a little added excitement. I knew I would be seeing Sallahdeen in a little while and I couldn't wait. Our first meetup didn't go as planned so hopefully today will be better. I don't know what it is about him but whatever it is has me going through the motions. He is the exact opposite of Haasan. I try not to compare them but its hard not to. From the start Sallahdeen and I hit it off. I can talk to him about anything. I wouldn't call him a funny guy but he makes me laugh. I feel good when I'm around him. And one thing I love is that he talks about the future and the plans that he has for himself. Which is something Haasan never does, he always talks about he lives in the present and he'll deal with the future in the future. That shit burns me up. Sallahdeen has admitted that his plans have been kind of on hold since his parents died. That's understandable, I was younger when my dad was killed so although it affected me, it was different. I still had my mom to guide me and continue with the foundation that had already been set. He lost both of his parents at the same time and he was a bit older. Although the circumstances are different we share the same sadness and pain and it is sort of comforting to talk to him knowing that he gets it. If you've never lost a parent I don't think you can relate to the pain and realize that grieving never ends. I mourn my dad every day and before meeting Sallahdeen, the only other person I could talk to freely about him was Manda. Not counting out my mom and Aunt Liv, but Manda and I have found that unless they bring up our dads we make no mention of them. I don't know, I can't really explain it but that's just how it has been the last couple of years.

Another way in which they are different is Haasan has different hustles to keep money in his pockets and since I've known him he has never held a job. Sallahdeen on the other hand told me that when he lived in Atlanta that he was a big brother- sort of a mentor throughout high school. In the summers, he worked at the camp that he used to attend when he was younger, as a counselor. He enjoyed working with the kids so much that he realized that's what he wanted to do, so he majored in education so that he could teach and in a way mentor. His plan was to get his Master's in Counseling but that came to a halt when…well you know. A man with a plan is so attractive to me, not to mention that he is so damn attractive. His swag is so on point, it's like---how do I explain it? He knows he looks good but he isn't arrogant with it. Whereas Haasan is one conceited dude and he is also very materialistic. I mean, I'm all about name brands but Haasan is a flaunter, he likes to show off. You'd think he was a damn Leo and not a Scorpio.

I can go on with more comparisons but the reality is that with Haasan I have to try and picture us together in the future and with Sallahdeen, there is no trying. I can actually see us together and building something really special. Just thinking about it makes my heart flutter-- in a good way.

Aunt Toni had yelled downstairs to see if I was home and I told her to hold up I'd be upstairs in a minute. She was making lunch and asked if I was hungry. *"Now you know I can always eat"*, I answered as I headed up the steps.

"Don't I know it?"

"What you making anyway?" I asked.

"Chicken and shrimp Alfredo, I been having a taste for it the last few days."

"Dang, you know I love your alfredo! Hook it up!"

She laughed. It was good to hear her laughing, it's been rare these days. I feel like she tries to put on a brave face for me but I know my aunt.

"So what's up with you nephew? What's been going on with you? Any little shorties you been entertaining? I'm sorry I've been kind of distant…"

"Auntie please, you don't have to apologize about anything. We're both trying to...get back to...normal."

She sighed, *"Yeah...normal...ughhh, why do I do this?!"* She seemed to be getting upset with herself.

"Why do you do what? Auntie, we both going through it, why you being so hard on yourself? And to answer your questions, not much, just trying to keep my head above the ground and yeah, its one little shorty."

She smiled, *"Oh yeah? Does this shorty have a name?"*

I smiled, *"Tovah."*

"Ohhh Tovah...you wanna tell me about this Tovah?"

"Well, it's not much to tell right now. But what I can tell you is that she is a nurse, she's gorgeous and she's feelin' ya boy", I started laughing.

"Damn, a nurse, I know that's right nephew. Get a girl that's on ya level, not one of these little hoes."

"Now come on auntie, hoes need love too." We both busted out laughing.

"Boy you crazy! When am I gonna meet this Tovah?"

I don't know…it's a bit complicated…"

"Oh, here we go. Why is it complicated?"

"She sort of got a boyfriend."

"Sort of? Either she do or she don't."

"She do, but it ain't like that. I mean, we vibe like crazy. She not happy with him."

"Deen, come on, I thought you knew better than that. Of course y'all vibin. That shit probably exciting to her, sneaking around and shit. And what if she do leave her boyfriend for you, you don't think she'll do the same thing to you?"

"It ain't like that auntie…and I do know better. This girl is just different…she's different than any girl I've ever dealt with."

"Sounds like somebody got the love bug…how long have you known her? You love this Tovah-girl Sallahdeen?"

"Only a couple of weeks. I don't know auntie, but she special, real special, and she do have me in my feelings. Maybe…we'll see."

"You know I been in these streets and I just want you to be careful. Especially since you don't really know her…or her boyfriend. There are two sides to a story and you only know hers. She could be playing you and just trying to get back at her man. Me and Nikki always told you that girls play the game just as much as y'all dudes- is all I'm saying. And these Philly dudes is just different."

"I hear you auntie." It's not often that Aunt Toni mentions my mom's name so I knew she was telling me to take heed to what she was saying.

"Okay nephew, you know your auntie just being straight like nine fifteen."

I busted out laughing, *"Oh you wanna quote Lil' Kim huh?"*

She cracked up laughing. Uncle George walked in the door. *"What's going on in here?"*

"Auntie in her bag Unc."

Aunt Toni said, *"Naw I'm just trying to school him about these females out here."*

"You better listen to her Deen, Toni knows the game and how it's played. We both do."

Aunt Toni gestured towards Uncle George and said, *"You heard him-listen to your uncle."*

Uncle George walked over to his wife and gave her a kiss then said *"Is that Alfredo I smell?"*

I answered, *"Yup, she cooking up some shrimp and chicken alfredo while feeding me some knowledge."*

Uncle George winked and smiled and said, *"that's my wife right there."*

"You better know it," she replied. *"Alright now go head babe, wash up, shower, do what you gotta do cause this food just about done."*

"That's my cue, I see y'all in a few" Uncle George said as he left out the kitchen.

Moments like this reminded me of times not too long ago when everything was good…when Mom and Pops was still alive. I haven't had too many good moments since they've been gone. But…hopefully things will be changing soon and I'll have a lot of good moments to look forward to.

Aunt Toni snapped her fingers and said, *"Hey, hey where you go cause you darn sure not here."*

I smiled, *"I'm back, just was thinking about something that's all."*

"You ready to eat or you gonna wait for George?"

Naw, I'll wait. I'm a go and get dressed cause I'm out after I eat."

"What you got somewhere to be?"

"Yeah, something like that."

"Uhm hmm."

I went downstairs and saw that I had two texts from Tovah. The first one asking was she going to see me and the next one telling me that she'll be at her mom's house until seven at the latest. I texted her back telling her that she'll see me and I slyly left out a specific time or any time for that matter.

After getting dressed, we all ate dinner together and I headed out to meet up with Tovah. Once in the car, my phone rang and Sam said he was going to Carlette's later and did I want to hang. I laughed and told him it was a plan and I'd holla at him later. I'm pretty sure that either way it go with Tovah, a drink might be what I need.

I pulled up at her mom's crib and Tovah's Audi was parked in the driveway. I never was a fan of Audi's, I don't see what the hype is about them. I was going to call her to let her know I was outside, but she came to the door like she was peeking through the blinds. I smiled and said, *"you was waiting on a nigga huh?"*

She laughed and said, *"Sure was."*

She put out her hand for me to take, so I took it and she escorted me in. I said, *"What's this, I'm getting some special treatment today?"*

"You sure are. And we just getting started. First, let's get one thing out of the way. Can I have my kiss?"

I didn't even answer her, I just pulled her close to me and kissed her like I've never kissed before. While I kissed her my dick just stood up and pressed into her. She seemed to like it but she pulled back. I pulled her back into another kiss and she pulled away and grasped my dick through my pants and said, *"That's for me?"*

I just bit my lip and nodded my head. She said, *"Tell me it's for me…say it."*

With no hesitation, I answered, *"It's for you."* Tovah never broke her stare as she loosened my belt and said, *"You just don't know how bad I've been wanting to do this."*

My dick seemed like it turned into a brick after she said that. It got so hard I was scared I was going to burst because I was too fucking excited. She slowly kissed me on my lips while running her hands up my shirt and across my chest, then she kissed my neck, she was driving me crazy! She went down further and started to pull my pants down and I assisted her. She got down on her knees and kissed my inner thighs. She finally put her hands on my rock hard dick that had already been standing and waiting for her. As she gripped it, it got even harder than it's ever been. She stroked it, then kissed it as she looked up at me. I turned away afraid that one glance might interrupt the pleasure that she was bestowing upon me. A gasp escaped my lips as my hand involuntarily settled in the back of her head while slightly pushing myself in her mouth and down her throat. She gagged and I looked down. She looked at me and smiled as she sucked my dick. She went hands free and began to suck harder as I started to fuck her mouth. As much as I didn't want her to stop I knew I was almost there, I couldn't control it. I told her that I was about to cum, I guess she didn't care because she just kept going. Within seconds I exploded in her mouth. I had to grab onto the chair that was nearby to keep myself from falling back. I shook my head and looked at Tovah, she stared me straight in my eyes as she licked her lips seductively. *"Damn"*, is all I could come up with. I barely had gotten myself together when Tovah put out her hand again and again I took it with no questions asked.

She led me up the steps, thankfully it was only a few because my legs felt all wobbly and shit. She took me into a bedroom which was easy to guess was hers when she lived here based on the big ass picture of her on the wall. She began to undress herself and when I came closer to help, she resisted. She was quiet and just looked at me. When she got down to just her panties and bra I felt the blood rushing to my dick again. When she turned her back towards me so that I could see she was wearing these sexy ass lace thongs, it was over. My dick was standing the fuck up and ready again. She bent over to take off the thongs and I couldn't help myself. I bent her over, grabbed a hold of her legs and spread em. I then kissed her butt cheeks before I slid my tongue between her lips and began to suck and chew on her clit. She was going crazy and it wasn't before long that I felt her warm juices in my mouth and over my face. I picked her up and put her on the bed and she was ready. If I put my dick in now it would be over before it started. So, I took off her bra and licked, sucked and bit any and every thing from her ears back to her pussy and to her toes. She begged for the dick and I pulled one of her numbers and said, *"tell me how bad you want it.'"* She obliged. My dick was wet from precum so I swirled my dick around her wet ass pussy and it was easy to enter. Her shit was so tight and warm and it had been a while since I had fucked, I was scared I was going to cum immediately. I was able to hold on but then as I stroked, long dicking her, I was looking her dead in the face and I felt her pussy tightening around my dick. She was about to cum and suddenly she kissed me so passionately that we both came together and she screamed. My body seemed to go limp because I felt like I couldn't move. I managed to at least get off of her and rolled over. We both lay there for a couple of minutes with nothing but heavy breathing to fill the silence. She finally turned her body towards mine and I did the same and we just smiled at each other.

It was our first time and I think it was better than either one of us had expected. I know it was better than I imagined. The next few weeks we continued to have our little rendezvous and each time seemed better than the last. She had even been over to my spot two or three times, but because we used the entrance downstairs Aunt Toni still hasn't met her. I don't know how much longer I could do this with Tovah because if I wasn't sure before, I'm sure now that

I am in love with her. And sharing her is no longer on the table.

These past couple of weeks have been kind of stressful for me, ever since the little *argument* if that's what you wanna call it with Haasan at the job that day. Argument is definitely not the right word, it was basically what it is- the truth and he showed that he couldn't handle the truth since he was left speechless. He had no comeback at all for me, so now he has been on my top and sneaking around with Sallahdeen has gotten a bit harder. Haasan is always in the streets, he's a hustler—his word not mine—so I guess being in the streets is a necessity. But, he's-- I guess trying to do better. It just that he's trying to be better a little too late. He pops up at the apartment more which is not unusual but he had slacked on it. He suggested that I stay over at his place last weekend because his homie Quaan had went away with his girlfriend. When I told Sallahdeen that I wouldn't talk to him for probably the whole weekend, he was pissed as hell. If I had to swear on it, I'd say he was teary-eyed. I mean he knew I had a boyfriend so…I'm acting nonchalant but I was sick about it too. Since I had started dealing with him, I don't think we've gone a day without at least texting. And since we started having sex, we talk every single day. If anybody looked through my phone they would think that Sallahdeen was my man and Haasan was the side jawn.

To say I was not looking forward to that weekend alone with Haasan would not be saying enough. But there was no way that I could back out. In the past I looked forward to time alone with him. Now, not so much. Since me and Sallahdeen been sleeping together I haven't had to have sex with Haasan because I was acting like I was so upset with him about neglecting me. I had used up all my plays with the card that the only time he pays me any mind is when he wants some. Another time he stayed over I was on my period so I had lucked up, but there was no reason or excuse that I could have come up with that could get me out of staying with him. He would have suspected something if I kept giving him excuses because in the past I have never been able to stay mad at him for too long.

I felt so weird just being with him lately. Knowing that I was falling for someone else made me uncomfortable when I was around him. It's like our conversations were so dry to me. Ever since I started seeing Sallahdeen, I saw that my relationship with Haasan was not up to par. We had no common interests for real and all we had was time in and good sex. And after that weekend you could scratch good sex too. It wasn't bad but it just wasn't *it* any more. I had always enjoyed sex with him because I didn't have anything to compare it to really. We had sex a few times throughout the weekend and the first time it was so awkward for me, I thought he felt it, but he didn't say anything. I have never faked enjoying sex, but that weekend I realized that I could be an actress. One time I even pictured Sallahdeen just to get through it and enjoy it. That helped a little bit but Sallahdeen was much bigger and with Sallahdeen if felt like we were making love and not just fucking. I didn't have to worry about screaming out the wrong name because I call them both either babe or baby, it's just easier. It's no way I could mistake him for Sallahdeen anyway because Haasan always fucked me like he was trying to destroy shit. His fucking skills were alright but I can't say shit about his pussy eating, he has that shit mastered. In fact, both of them are very good at that shit but in different ways. That's probably why Haasan couldn't tell any difference because his foreplay was always to eat my pussy then jump right into sex. No matter how much my mind and body seemed to now belong to Sallahdeen, it seemed my pussy had a mind of its own and was up for grabs.

The weekend was just a long drag out of Netflix and chill. We ate, watched TV, fucked slept and repeat. We both had our phones on silent, I was cool with that just in case Sallahdeen tried to call or text but surprisingly he didn't. I know he was heated. Haasan just wanted to make sure he didn't miss any money but said that he told I guess who needed to be told that he would be unavailable that weekend.

By Sunday morning he was ready to call it quits on our weekend. He had made us some breakfast and while we were eating asked would I be upset if we end our weekend a bit earlier than what we decided. I told him that was fine. He said he might need to go out of town in the next few days, he'll let me know as soon as he know. I saw him check his phone Saturday night when we were in bed and whatever or whoever it was you could tell he was a little irritated that he missed it. I asked him then was he okay and he said he was cool.

After we ate I went to shower, ready to get back home and when I got out he was in the bedroom waiting for me dick standing tall. I thought I would get away without fucking him again but no dice. I acted like I wanted it and asked, *"Is that for me?"* he nodded his head smiling and I hopped on his dick and rode it until he came. I'm pretty sure he wanted me to suck it first but naw that wasn't happening. He seemed happy which he always was when I rode him. I rode him with my back facing him so he couldn't see me rolling my eyes all the while talking shit to him while he was telling me I got the best pussy.

The past two weeks I been trying to redeem myself from that day with Tovah. I've been trying to spend as much time as I can with her and she seemed at first to be giving me her ass to kiss. But I think I'm softening her up even though she not letting me fuck. My homie Quaan was going away for the weekend with his girl Kayla, so I suggested that she spend the weekend over at my spot so we can have some alone time together. The weekend was going alright, I had went to the market and got some food for us, I bought me a bottle and we had the Firestick so we could just chill and spend some much needed time together. I figured this is what she been asking for so why not. I'm trying to do whatever I can to please her. I even suggested that we put our phones on silent for the whole weekend. She said why not turn them off but I told her I wasn't trying to miss any money. I wasn't lying.

I've always been somewhat unclear to Tovah as to what I do to make money. I think that she has always believed that I was a drug dealer, I mean she wouldn't be wrong. I dibbled and dabbled in a bunch of things which is why I just tell her I'm a hustler by nature and getting money is what I do. She never seemed pressed which is funny because she is newsy as shit! That's why I look at her different from other chicks I've fucked around with. They be all up in your business and be pressed to find out how you getting money or who you getting money with. Lately though, she'd be surprised to find out how I get money and the kind of money

I'm getting. Which is why my phone being turned off wasn't an option.

Our weekend was going good, as planned. I had her going crazy as usual. The first time we had sex, she seemed to be holding back like she ain't want it, but I know my tongue game does the trick every time. It loosened her up and she was giving it to me as usual. Her shit is so good, I don't know what I been thinking. I can't even imagine, shit don't want to even think about her giving this shit to somebody else. Spending this time with her brought me back to my senses and I realized that I have been taking her for granted and I'm gon do better. I probably sound soft and shit but I miss us being like this even though I know it's my fault that shit started changing.

Throughout the weekend I only checked my phone a couple times but when I checked my phone on Saturday night I saw that I had a text from Ralph. That means he got some work for me. I figured I'd be hearing from him soon, I just didn't know when, it's been a while. I usually get an empty text from him about once every six weeks or so. That's how he works. I get the text and go pay him a visit within the next twenty four hours. So it looks like I'm gonna have to cut it short with Tovah. I figured I'd tell her in the morning.

For the past year or so, I've gotten eight texts from Ralph exactly the same way. My brother put me on...I don't know if that's a good shout out or not, but it's a fact. I love my brother and proved that I would do anything for him. About two years ago I paid a debt -more like a favor -that he owed some old head Ralph. Afterwards he came to me with a proposition that I really had to think about. The money was real fucking good and I would be set and so would Shaheed. He made it sound so easy. And I gotta admit, it was easy. But I wasn't sure, look where he ended up. He doing a twenty year bid, he built for that prison shit, I'm not. He thinks that I proved that I'm just as ruthless as he is though, shit he actually seemed like he was surprised. We got the same blood running through our veins, so it shouldn't have been that big of a surprise. I guess because I always was a momma's boy. I wonder where that shit come from though, it gotta be mom's family because ain't shit rough or ruthless about my dad and he never gave us no indication that he was ever about that life.

Just thinking back to that night…I was given a name, shit not even a government, just a nickname and a picture the week before. I drove down to Baltimore and went to the strip club that I was told I could find the bol in the picture and sure enough he was there. I was kind of surprised when he came in that he didn't have an entourage or something. I mean, I didn't know shit about him. I just figured that since somebody wanted him dead he must be important or something. He didn't even look the type. I guess I was expecting a thug looking muthafucka, his presence wasn't even threatening.

I sat at a table, had a couple of shots and even enjoyed a lap dance from a shorty that seemed pressed. I guess to her I was a new face which meant new money. I'm sure it was her job to know the regulars. What was her name, Diamond? Yeah that was her name -Diamond, she was a baddie and under any other circumstances I probably would've fucked in her the truck I had rented, but I was there with one purpose and that was to kill this dude named Black.

I left out the club a little after midnight and waited in the truck for him to come out. He came out close to one and you could tell he was lit walking to his car stumbling and shit. He had started the car with his automatic starter as soon as he exited the club and then dropped his keys while standing at the driver's door. When he bent down to pick them he was startled to see me standing there. He looked confused probably wondering who the fuck I was and before he could say anything I shot him twice in the dome. I didn't wait to watch him drop. I got in the truck, got on I-95N and headed back to Philly. I had just killed somebody and it didn't faze me one bit.

The next morning I visited my brother and told him that his debt was paid. He looked genuinely shocked but smiled. He asked me how I felt. I told him it was nothing to me, I was cool. He asked me do I think I could do it again and I answered 'without hesitation'.

Shaheed finally convinced me that this was better than trapping. That shit was only getting me petty money anyway and it damn sure wasn't building my bank account. I hear the stories from the old heads talking about how they was getting it back in the day but these same muthafuckas don't have shit to show for it. The few niggas I heard that was really getting it back then ain't nowhere to be seen or heard from. They disappeared and with good reason. The first chance these broke ass dudes get they going to try to take them for whatever they can. My homie Quaan brother got rich off of trappin and turned all that drug money legal. Unfortunately for him, a few bum ass niggas broke in his house while him, his girl and baby was asleep. He woke up to three niggas in his bedroom with a gun pointed to each of their heads. He had no choice but to show them his safe.

They got what they wanted but they still killed him and his

girl and left the baby alive in the crib. Word on the street was

that it was his own homie who was on some hatin, jealous

shit. If it was or wasn't, that same homie was found dead not

even a week later. These streets is vicious and I'm not trying

to get caught up.

I've been doing this shit for the past year and a half

and I've made me more money than I ever did selling drugs

and I been doing that since I was young bol. I ain't have to

trap, it was just something to do, shit just about everybody

was doing it and what young bol wouldn't want a few extra

dollars in their pockets? Like I said before, the old head

Ralph gives me a name and a picture and tells me where I

most likely can find them. Don't nobody know about this shit

except my brother. Raoul thinks that Ralph be giving me

weight to push. It's not too many people you can let know

that you're a hit man for hire. Basically, I'm just taking over

where my brother left off. Of course as a young bol I didn't know this was what he was into. Shaheed got me by eleven years so that comes as no surprise that I didn't know my brother was out here killing shit-literally. First time I found out about it was when he asked me to do him that favor. At first I thought he was shittin' me. When I realized he wasn't, I couldn't believe it, but I think he was testing me at the same time. I always looked up to him growing up, I wanted to be fly just like he was. Who would've known that I'd be following in his footsteps like for real? I just don't plan on ending up where he at though. I don't think I could do it- real talk. Crazy thing, that's not even why he locked up though. He got jammed up on an attempted murder charge. His daughter's mom had an ex who was abusive and was pissed that she had moved on with Shaheed and was having Shaheed's baby. He rode up on her coming out of a store and jumped out the car yelling at her and shit and grabbing her. Little did he know my brother was in the store which was a big mistake for him. When Shaheed realized what was going on he came out the store and began pistol whipping him. He said he was so fucking mad he couldn't stop and didn't care about any witnesses. A few of those same witnesses testified against him and said that he was trying to kill bol and no one stepped in to help because they feared he might shoot them with the gun he was using to beat the bol. He was arrested at the scene and been locked up ever since. As a result of the beating the bol's mouth was wired shut, I heard he lost his hearing or some shit and was blind in one eye. My bro fucked him up and fucked his self up too. Twenty years though? I can't even imagine doing that type of time.

Shaheed always talking that shit like how it's so easy to get away with murder, man he get off on that shit. He be so happy to talk about the bodies he got, that shit be so weird to me. It's like he living his life all over again through me. I mean I can't judge because I'm doing the same shit he was doing. I'on know, maybe because I'm new to this...or maybe I just don't get the same satisfaction as Shaheed does being a cold-hearted killer. Either way, work is calling and it's time to make the donuts.

I called Tovah earlier and told her that we needed to talk and in person. I'm usually straightforward and open but I was acting a bit secretive so she couldn't help but to ask what was up. I told her I'd let her know once I see her. The conversation I wanted to have with her needed to happen in person. It was time for all this sneaking around to end. She's told me that she doesn't see a future with her current boyfriend so I don't get what's the point of staying with him.

I had all I could take from this whole situation last week. Tovah told me that she put it all out on the table with her boyfriend that shit wasn't right between them. I'm like okay cool. But then after she told him that it became hard for me because he was trying to get his shit right with her because of what she had said to him. I had gotten so used to seeing her but now I got put on the back burner. I have never been a side jawn and I have found that shit is absolutely not for me. It all came to a head for me when she said that she was spending the weekend over his house because he said they need some quality time and that she would be out of reach until Monday when she goes to work. I can't even explain how I was going through it the whole weekend. Just knowing that she was fucking somebody else made me sick to my stomach. I know I did this shit to myself fucking with a bitch that got a man. Not calling Tovah a bitch cause that's my baby.

If after this conversation she doesn't make a decision, she won't have to, I will make it for her. I have fallen so hard for this girl and I can't keep doing this shit to myself. She has even admitted that she loves me too so that makes it worse. Two and a half months, damn near three months that's all it's been. I didn't think I could ever be this happy especially so soon after my parents died. Tovah makes me happy, really happy- but don't get it fucked up I will walk away if I have to.

If my parents taught me anything, it's that I am deserving of whatever I want and don't ever settle for less. And, I'm not.

Ever since I stayed with Haasan, shit has been different with me and Sallahdeen and definitely not for the better. I mean I'm not surprised because if the roles were reversed I don't think I could handle it. The type of man that Sallahdeen is I could guess that it was a hit to his manhood. Once I started really getting to know him, I told him that I was surprised that he was even fucking with me. He told me that he thought I was worth it. But, I think he is starting to regret putting himself in this situation.

I reached out to him the same day I left Haasan's and he didn't respond. When we finally spoke, he was very nonchalant. You could tell he was feeling some kind of way but was trying to act normal. Our conversation was not the same. He was getting me back whether it was on purpose or not. Now I was sick because I missed him. I didn't know how to fix this. Haasan hasn't been around either. The next day he came over and told me he would be out of town for the next few days because he had business to take care of and then was going to see Shaheed afterwards. He tried to get some that night and I told him my pussy was sore from the weekend. I was hoping to see Sallahdeen while he was out of town but the way things were going that probably wouldn't happen. Tonight was the night I agreed to work for Joanie and I should be trying to get a nap in but I wasn't sleepy. I would probably sleep all day tomorrow.

Manda popped her head in the door, *"Tov you alright? You been moping around the house and staying in your room and shit, I miss you big head."*

"I know cousin, I just don't know what to do. I miss himmmm" I said in a whiny voice.

"Yeah…I don't know, I can't call this one. When the last time you heard from him?"

Just as she asked the question my phone went off and it was Sallahdeen. I put my phone screen towards her so that she could see. She said, *"Good luck"* and walked away.

I answered the phone, *"Hey stranger."*

"Hey beautiful, you busy?"

"No, never for you," I answered and then rolled my eyes at myself (as I remembered I was just busy all last weekend *and* out of touch). He was probably thinking the same thing. I continued with *"what's up?"*

He said what I have been dreading, *"we need to talk."*

I said, *"Yeah...we do."*

"In person. We need to talk in person. Are you free now?"

I hesitated then answered, *"Well, yeah, I work tonight but I can shower real quick and be ready in about an hour or even forty-five minutes."*

"Oh that's tonight? Okay, sounds good. Did you eat yet?"

"Actually no, but I could eat something light." I lied hoping that he would feel sorry for me, *"I haven't had much of an appetite the past few days."*

"Oh word? So, since you work tonight I can pick you up and drop you off at work if that's cool for you…just so we don't have to double back, it don't make sense for us to drive two cars."

"Okay, no, I hear you, that's fine."

"Alright, see you soon" he said and then hung up.

I sat there for a second unsure what to think because he talking about he needs to talk to me in person? But then, he wants to drive together which seems to be a good sign because if he was dumping me he wouldn't want to drive back together, right? I don't know. I'm just happy that I'm about to see him, it's only been days but it seems much longer.

I showered and was ready to go in about thirty five minutes. I sat in the living room with Manda probably blowing her high with all my speculating about my talk with Sallahdeen. She just sat there puffing on her el and nodding her head. Sallahdeen texted me saying he would be to me in about two minutes. It's crazy that this will be the first time that he's been in front of my place and according to how this conversation goes it might be the last.

I saw him pull up, gave Manda a quick kiss on the cheek, said *'love you'* and was out.

My homie Shawn had called me out of the blue and said he was in town- only for the night though. Shawn was a cool ass Italian dude who it that seems like I've known forever. We were friends as far back that I could remember. We lived on the same block growing up all the way up to high school. I think it was freshman year that his step pop and mom bought a house over Jersey and they moved him and his little brothers out of his Aunt's house. I would still see him from time to time but he started this boxing thing that took off after high school so you know how that goes. Whenever he comes to Philly though he makes sure to reach out and either it's a hit or miss. When it hits we hang out, catch up and talk about us back in the day as young bols, it's always love.

Just so happen he called me on my drive back from the prison and said that he was in town to check out a fight club or some shit and asked was I free. I told him it was his lucky night and that I was on the road and probably bout an hour from where he was. He said one of his friends told him about a spot in Willow Grove and we could meet up there. We agreed to meet up in an hour.

I called Tovah but the phone just rang. I remembered she mentioned something about working the night shift so she was probably sleep. Since she's off tomorrow, maybe I'll take her out to dinner and spend some quality time with her. I haven't seen her in a few days and I'm trying to stay on her good side. I been on her top lately and don't have no plans on slowing down. Last weekend was cool, we had fun, and it seemed like old times. So, yeah dinner tomorrow is the plan.

I pulled up to the address that Shawn gave me and it was a restaurant. I had just assumed it was a bar but good thing because I could eat something. All I had was those vending machine wings and the shit they be having in the visiting rooms. I had got there before Shawn so I went and sat at the bar and just looked around and thought that maybe

I'd bring Tovah here tomorrow. I had to see what the food was hitting for first though. I see Shawn walking my way, he must've spotted me first because he had this big ass grin on his face.

"Yooo look at you all buff and shit."

Shawn laughed and bear hugged me, *"My man Haasan, it's good to see you man! What the fuck is up?"*

"Damn, nigga, I could barely breathe and shit", I laughed.

"I know, you see this shit," he said while flexing both of his biceps.

"Aw man get the fuck outta here!"

"So what's been up man? I see you still on your pretty boy shit."

"Well, you know what can I say?" I said as I rubbed my chin.

"What's up with your bro? He good? You know I got you or him if you ever need me."

"Yo, I appreciate that, real talk. He asked me if I heard from you a few weeks back, I'm a let him know you asked about him. And that's where I'm coming from. Taking that four hour drive."

"Oh shit, for real?! Four hours?"

"Yup, I'm up there at least three, four times a month ain't shit changed. But, he good. What you got for me? Any news, wedding bells or some shit. How long you and Deanna been together?"

"Ahh, I know you not talking, what's up with Sheena, naw not Sheena- Tovah? What's up wit her y'all been together what like four, five years? "

"Oh you wild, talking about Sheena, you know that shit been over like three years ago."

We went back and forth fucking with each other while catching up. I bussed a serious grub while he ate a fucking salad and drank water. Talkin' bout he on some boxer diet. We chilled for damn near two hours and I told him to hit me up with the date of his next fight. We hugged it out and both walked to our cars.

Now I know my fucking eyes are deceiving me. A truck drove by and I could have sworn that I saw Tovah in the passenger seat. As I walked to my car I called her phone. She didn't pick up. Okay, that don't mean nothing because she might be sleep or getting dressed for work tonight. I'll call her again in a few or wait for her to call me back. Better yet, I'll make my way to her spot. I know that wasn't her, I'm trippin'. And who was bol? I didn't even get a look at him I just so happened to see a truck with tint and took notice. The shit I be out here doing I can get a little paranoid sometimes. I jumped on the e-way, I should be there in bout twenty minutes tops. It's a thirty-five minute drive but the way I'm driving shit it might take fifteen if I don't get pulled over first.

I get to the block and see her car parked out front. I knew that wasn't her. I'm trippin. I get out the car and walk up and ring the doorbell. Manda answered and tried to hide that she looked shocked. "What's up Manda?" I said as I started to get in the door like any other time.

"What up Haasan?" She said while kind of blocking the door.

"You gon let me in or what?" I could feel myself getting irritated.

"Tov not here, she had to work tonight."

"What you mean she not here? Her car still parked out front. How the fuck she get to work?"

"Man, I don't fuckin know, I think a Lyft or something."

I pushed passed Manda and went straight to Tovah's bedroom not knowing what the fuck I was gon find. "What the fuck Haasan?!" Manda yelled after me. She wasn't in her bedroom.

"Since when the fuck she don't drive to work?!

"Something wrong with her car, I don't know. Ask her when you see her."

"Oh, I'ma ask her alright. I'm on my way to see her now. So you mind as well fucking call her and let her know I'm on my fucking way!"

"Yo, Haasan you trippin'." Manda said.

"Yeah, aiight, I'm trippin'," I said as I left back out the door.

I jumped in my car and headed straight to her job. I know Tovah ain't out here cheating on me. I banged on the steering wheel. All I could see was red! I gotta calm the fuck down. I got back on the e-way and got bout ten minutes before I get to Jefferson. I just kept saying to myself 'calm down'. Car trouble? Get the fuck out of here. I talked to her and she ain't say shit about no car trouble. "Calm down." I had never put my hands on any female...man, I need to calm down. I called her phone again, it went straight to voicemail.

"Oh this bitch playin wit me?! I know she saw my call. She wit a nigga and ain't pickin up for me? For me?!"

A few blocks from Jefferson and all I hear is Raoul in my ear, 'bitches be in whole other relationships and their niggas be clueless'. Is that what I am? A clueless nigga? Naw…I don't even know what's going on. I might be trippin. But I'm about to find out. I'm at the light and I see the same truck that I thought I saw Tovah in parked out front of the entrance to the ER. I pull over just to see what's what. The car was still running and the tint on the car not that dark so I can see that it's two people in there.

After about two minutes, the driver got out and walked to the passenger side and opened the door. What a fuckin gentleman! Next, out steps fuckin Tovah! I sat there just to see what the fuck was gonna happen. This nigga gripped my girl by the waist and pulled her close to him and I watched them as they kissed like they were a couple and I was the side nigga watching salty as shit. That's how I felt.

My blood was fuckin boiling! I sat there and couldn't believe what I was seeing. I watched as Tovah went in the entrance and turned back to him one last time smiling and waving. I'll deal with her later.

I waited for him to get back in the car and I followed him to see who this dude was. After a few minutes, I figured he was going to the casino because that's the way he was going. Instead he double parked near The Punch Line. I drove by him but not too far where I couldn't see him. It wasn't crowded at all outside and he seemed to be waiting for somebody. I don't recognize him at all. Who the fuck is this dude? The bol came out and I recognized him as some lame ass nigga, the fuck is his name? Sam. Always been a wannabe down ass nigga. He hit the lottery or some shit and got a whole gang of friends now. Tovah fucking around on me with a lame ass nigga?! He about to find out he fuckin with the wrong one and she got a real ass nigga!

I got out my car and started walking towards them. They laughing and shit not even paying attention. The nigga ought to know better, niggas been on his top trying rob him and shit. He lucky I'm on some other shit tonight because he could have ended up in my fucking trunk duct taped, roped and wrapped up. When I finally caught their attention, I knew immediately that the bol Sam recognized me because he looked at the bol. The bol looked at me and smiled. Not even smiled, it was more of a smirk. Did this pussy ass nigga just smile at me?! Wait, do he know who the fuck I am?! The fuck he think this is? He got me all the way fucked up! I took my gun out my waist and shot him. I shot him and at the bol Sam even though I don't know where I hit him at. I ran to the car and sped off. I don't even remember how many shots I got off but I know I dropped that pussy that smiled at me. Sam surprised me, I slept on him and he was strapped too. He was just shooting and shit and hit me in the shoulder I'm starting to feel that shit now. I see what niggas be talking bout, that shit burn like a muthafucka. Damn what that motherfucker hit me with? I gotta slow down I feel like I'm bout to pass out. Just as the thought entered my head, I swerved, I tried to control the car but I couldn't keep my eyes open. Fuck!

I don't how long I was out but I woke up to fucking ambulance sirens. Shit! I smashed my car into a stop sign. Fuck is that smell? The air bags. What the fuck? I know the cops will be here soon. Right as the ambulance pulled up I noticed my gun on the floor. I reached for it and winced in pain. My fucking chest hurt. What I broke a rib or something? I managed to put it behind my back in my waistband. How the fuck I'ma get out of this? I opened the driver's door and went to get out and I damn near fell. The EMT's ran over to assist me and one sat me down leaning against the car calling me sir? I felt a little disoriented. I must be sweating real bad, the dude wiped my forehead and asked was I okay? Fuck no. Do I know my name? Yeah. The other one came back with a first aid kit and put a bandage on my head. I must be bleeding. They asked did I hurt anywhere. Yeah, everywhere. They telling me that they're about to lift me onto a gurney and would be taking me to the hospital. Shit. They hooked me to an IV. I nodded back off. I woke up again head feeling clearer than before. We arrived at the hospital, Jefferson Emergency Room I saw as they opened the doors. The EMT's took me in and told the people that I was in a car crash. Dumb motherfuckers were still unaware that I'd been shot. For a quick second I thought that I just might be able to sneak out before anybody realize. I'm pretty sure that one of them niggas was brought here DOA I hope. Then I overheard somebody whispering asking if the cops were notified. Fuck, fuck, fuck!! They knew.

I gotta figure what the fuck to do. I can't go to jail for no double murder! I'll be damned. That shit must be in our fucking blood! Same way Shaheed got jammed up over a bitch! Man fuck Tovah, where the fuck she at anyway?! The curtain opens and walks in a nurse, I've seen her before but she don't recognize me. She asked me how I am feeling and then asked if she could take a look at my shoulder. She looked at it and told me I was lucky that it just missed my clavicle because that would be painful and would take longer

to heal. I asked her why I wasn't really feeling any pain and

before she answered the curtain pulls back and in comes

Tovah.

I keep calling Tovah's phone but the shit just keeps ringing, she probably got her shit on vibrate. I always get on her about that shit because her phone can be right in her damn pocket and she don't even feel it. If Haasan get to her before I do, who knows what the fuck gonna happen! I ain't never see him like that before. I gotta let her know that he is on his way to her. I hope she not still with the bol. Man, fuck sitting here keep calling her phone, I gotta get to Jefferson to make sure she cool.

The night so far had been slow thankfully for me because all I could think about was what happened before I had gotten to work. Sallahdeen had suggested we get something to eat before my shift and we went to what had become *our spot* for a quick bite. I told him I didn't want to eat too much and then be sluggish all night. He told me that he really needed to talk to me about something. I was curious what he wanted to talk about in person rather than on the phone. He asked if it was cool for him to pick me up from home and said that he would drive me to work and pick me up in the morning. I told him that was cool, I knew that Haasan would be out of town until at least tomorrow.

On the way to the restaurant I could see that he was antsy which made me all the more curious of what was going on. We got there, ordered our food and Sallahdeen finally said, *"I guess you wondering what I want to talk to you about?"*

"You know I am. This is definitely not like you, you're always straight to the point. What's going on?"

"I know, I got to admit I'm a little nervous". Now my interest was piqued. He was nervous?

He began by saying, "what it's been damn near three months that we been doing this, seeing each other?" I shook my head in agreement. "It's been mostly fun and all...amazing actually" He hesitated and my heart dropped. Was he about to tell me we were over? He began again and was serious as hell when he asked, "Tov, do you love me?"

I answered him, "you know I do, but..."

"But what? You love me and you know how much I love you. I told you before, I have never felt this way before about anybody. And, I'm done hiding how I feel. I want you to be MY woman. I can't take this shit no more".

"Sallahdeen, where is this coming from? Everything has been perfect with us, why are you trying to mess us up?"

"You can't be serious? Us? There is no us. You call me knowing that another man has been able to kiss you, feel you, be inside you perfect then you not as smart as I know you are. You got me fucked up and I know you feel the same way. Shit, when I told you that the jawn Lucky was trying holla at me, you flipped the fuck out. I put my head down and just shook my head. "What?" he asked.

"What do you expect me to do? Just break up with him just like that? You think he's gonna let me go just like that? I said while snapping my fingers. It's complicated because I do have feelings for him".

"Are you in love with him?" he asked. I wasn't but it's still not that easy to just let Haasan go. I answered, "No, I'm in love with you Sallahdeen, but…"

"But what? That's all that matters that we love each other. Ain't shit complicated about that." He put his hand on *my chin and made me look up at him, "Tov, I know it's not gonna be easy, but why would stay in a relationship with him and you're telling me you love me? Is this a game to you?"*

"What?! No, why would you say that?" I asked defensively.

"I'm not a fool. I love you and I don't want to hide that anymore, okay? And I won't go through what I went through last weekend ever again."

"Baby, I told you I'm sorry."

"Don't be sorry, leave that nigga...or lose me."

My eyes started to fill with tears. "I can't lose you Sallahdeen, I love you baby."

He smiled that beautiful smile of his and kissed my tears as they fell. I tucked my bottom lip in and nodded my head to let him know I agree with what he has been saying. I knew what I had to do. He kissed me lightly and then again gently forcing his tongue in my mouth and kissed me so

passionately as if to seal our conversation with a kiss.

"Damn girl, what you thinking about?"

"Oh hey, what's up Chuck, long time no see"? Chuck

was one of the overnight transports who I used to sometimes

bust it up with when I worked the overnights.

He laughed and said, *"You was gone, smiling and*

shit. I'm good though, I can't complain. I see you still all in

love huh?"

I just smiled and said, *"That's what's up and*

whatever". Shit, if he only knew I'm in love alright, just not

with Haasan. I know I told Sallahdeen that I didn't wanna

lose him but I don't know how to do this. I mean I am in love

with him and I love Haasan. I just don't know how to handle

this. I'm tired of sneaking around even though it hasn't been

as hard as I always thought it would be. Haasan really has

been slacking lately, he probably out here doing the same

thing I'm doing that's why it's been so easy for me. Over

these past few months, I had a couple close calls or lies that could've almost got me caught up but other than that I have been having damn near a whole relationship and this nigga didn't even realize. Sallahdeen is right, it's time for us to be together. Me and Haasan's relationship is over I just had to admit it and he is gonna have to face it too. Interrupting my realization and thoughts was the charge nurse announcing that there were two gunshot victims arriving and were six and nine minutes out. Everyone was on alert and began making necessary preparations for the incoming patients.

My task was to assist on the first incoming ambulance. Hearing the ambulance siren getting close I waited at the emergency room entrance ready to assist. This is the one thing I didn't miss about working on the overnights. You never knew what you were going to see in the ER. I'll never forget my first gunshot patient, nobody could ever prepare you for it either. I never got used to seeing it and then hearing the cries of the families of those who were shot and as a result died--was by far the worst thing.

Mornings were busier but you'd likely see more sick people than victims of crimes on that shift. I'd take that any day.

The first ambulance pulled in and the EMT that was driving got out stating that the patient was a young black male with a gunshot wound to the abdomen and the chest. As the doors in the back of the ambulance opened the other EMT said that he had begun to crash. They pulled out the gurney and on it was Sallahdeen.

As I ran along the side of the gurney, I was trying to make sense of what I was seeing. It felt like a nightmare. I kept telling him that everything was going to be alright. I didn't realize that I was actually yelling at Sallahdeen that he has to be okay. The EMT was on top of him administering CPR and just stopped. I began to yell at him asking why did he stop and he just looked at me with this distressing look that I recognized all too well. This was not happening. This was a fucking nightmare!

Before it could sink in that Sallahdeen had just died right in front of my eyes, my attention went to the second ambulance that had just arrived. I don't know what I was expecting to see or who I was expecting to see but it was Sallahdeen's homie, Sam. He had been shot once in the shoulder and was going to be okay. I yelled at him asking what the hell happened and who do this them. He said, "Your boyfriend. Your boyfriend pulled up on the both of us and didn't even say anything. Him and Deen kind of just smiled at each other and then he pulled out his gun and started shooting. I managed to get off a shot, I know I got him I just don't know where. Then he jumped in his car and took off." I couldn't believe what I was hearing. I didn't understand. *"What do you mean? Haasan? Haasan did this? But that doesn't make any sense."*

"Yeah that's his name. Haasan with the black tinted Infiniti right?"

"Yeah, but he didn't...he's out of town, he couldn't of..." I was trying to make sense of this and couldn't come up with anything. *Haasan killed Sallahdeen? Did he know about us? How long has he known? Why didn't he say anything? Naw, this is not true, it don't make any sense. Haasan would've definitely said something to me if he suspected or knew that I was dealing with Sallahdeen or anyone.* Chuck came over to me and asked if I was alright. I just looked at him and said *"this doesn't make any sense"*.

He said *"Tovah, can I call someone for you?"*

"Manda, please get Manda" I can hear myself saying.

Next thing I hear is that a car crash victim was coming in. I tried to focus but all that my thoughts could muster up was that Sallahdeen was dead and Haasan is the person that killed him. Jamie, one of the nurses, tapped me on the shoulder and said, "I got the next one Tovah, why don't you go to the locker room and get yourself together". I didn't realize that I was standing in the middle of the ER with tears streaming down my face. I didn't go to the locker room, I went to the room where Sallahdeen's body still lay and just stared at him. I was just with him. *How is this even real life?* I walked over to him and touched his hand which was still warm. I grasped his hand tighter. I kissed his lips and told him I loved him as the tears continued to fall. Just then two guys came into the room and I recognized one of them as the transport for the morgue. Neither of them said anything, they just looked apologetically at me. I had to get out of there, I couldn't be in there to see them place a sheet over Sallahdeen's body. I walked out of the room wiping my face with the back of my hands. I went back to the area where Sam was so I could tell him that Sallahdeen was dead.

"Tovah, I know, I knew when I heard you screaming and you confirmed it when I saw you the first time. I already called his Uncle, him and his Aunt Toni are on their way here now. I can't believe Deen is gone, this shit crazy." I couldn't believe it. I just walked without saying anything.

As I walked down the hall, I heard a familiar voice coming from behind one of the curtains. I hesitated, but I pulled the curtain back and there was Haasan. I stood there stuck just staring at him. He stared back with this sort of devilish smirk. Jamie, the nurse asked us both were we okay. I couldn't seem to form any words so Haasan spoke up and asked if we could have some privacy. Jamie looked at me to confirm it was okay for her to leave and I shook my head that it was okay although I'm sure my face looked terrified. Haasan said, *"What's up babe, you don't seem to be happy to see me?"* I tried to remain calm but I was anything but. I walked over to him and stuttered, *"H-hey babe, I thought you were in a car accident? It looks like you were shot though"*. *"Damn, that's not the reaction, I thought I would get from you Tovah. You don't even seem surprised. I was in a car accident after I was shot by your boyfriend's homie"*. He was looking me dead in my eyes waiting for a reaction. Nothing. He grabbed me by the wrist and said in a whisper, *"Yeah, I killed your boyfriend"*! I felt like I couldn't breathe. All I *could think was that it's true when they say everything that's done in the dark always comes to the light. But damn, I would have never thought that it would be like this!* Haasan held on tighter to my wrist with one hand and held a gun that I was just noticing unsteady with his other hand. *"How could you do this to me? Who them tears for?! That nigga?! You love that nigga?"*

"Baby, I'm s-" I stammered.

"You what? Sorry? Fuck that! You been out here playing me? You was fucking bol?! He looked at me with a look that I had never seen on his face. I was terrified. At that moment in the distance I heard the cops asking where were the shooting victims that had been brought in. I was praying that Haasan hadn't heard but he had. That seemed to only make his grip on my wrist even tighter. I said, *"Haasan, you're hurting me."* He held the gun steady and said, *"I'm sorry baby, you brought this shit on yourself."*

"Baby, please, please don't do this", I pleaded.

He stared me directly in my eyes and said, *"You did this"*. As tears fell from his eyes he pulled the trigger.

THE END